THE PRISONER OF
HELL GATE

A Novel

Dana I. Wolff

PICADOR

NEW YORK

THE PRISONER OF HELL GATE. Copyright © 2016 by Verbitrage LLC, Series I. All rights reserved. Printed in the United States of America. For information, address Picador, 175 Fifth Avenue, New York, N.Y. 10010.

picadorusa.com • picadorbookroom.tumblr.com
twitter.com/picadorusa • facebook.com/picadorusa

Picador® is a U.S. registered trademark and is used by St. Martin's Press under license from Pan Books Limited.

For book club information, please visit facebook.com/picadorbookclub or e-mail marketing@picadorusa.com.

Designed by Greg Collins

Library of Congress Cataloging-in-Publication Data

Names: Wolff, Dana I., author.
Title: The prisoner of Hell Gate : a novel / Dana I. Wolff.
Description: New York : Picador, 2016.
Identifiers: LCCN 2015044379 (print) | LCCN 2016001775 (e-book) | ISBN 9781250089700 (paperback) | ISBN 9781250089717 (e-book)
Subjects: LCSH: Typhoid Mary, -1938—Fiction. | Hell Gate (New York, N.Y.)—Fiction. | Horror fiction. | BISAC: FICTION / Historical. | FICTION / Horror. | FICTION / General.
Classification: LCC PS3623.O558 P75 2016 (trade paperback) | LCC PS3623.O558 (e-book) | DDC 813/.6—dc23
LC record available at http://lccn.loc.gov/2015044379

Our books may be purchased in bulk for promotional, educational, or business use. Please contact your local bookseller or the Macmillan Corporate and Premium Sales Department at 1-800-221-7945, extension 5442, or by e-mail at MacmillanSpecialMarkets@macmillan.com.

First published as an e-original by Picador

First Picador Paperback Edition: July 2016

10 9 8 7 6 5 4 3 2 1

Dana I. Wolff is the pseudonym of a former publishing executive who has also worked as a literary agent and entrepreneur. *The Prisoner of Hell Gate* is the first Wolff novel.

In memory of
Peter James Horoszko, *editor,*
gone before his time

All life exists at the expense of other life
Because you have eaten and eat as eat you must
—Frank Bidart, "The Third Hour of the Night"

As there is a God in Heaven I will get justice, somehow, sometime.
—Mary Mallon, 1909

THE PRISONER OF HELL GATE

Mary

BROTHERS SHE HAD once, but none so suffocating as this Brother.

It is a stifling September night. The summer does not relent. Dampness prevails, as always, but at this time less from the river and more from the mugginess that weighs on everything. It penetrates the very bricks, their crumbling mortar spongy to the touch.

The lettuces in the greenhouse sag under it. Under its weight, the shreds of old window canopies hang from desolate buildings like the fingers of discarded gloves.

More worrisome, the human souls who share her island float over the disused pier, glowing in the night, and she is their only witness. They yawp yawp yawp, chittering for help.

As if. They are long past earthly assistance.

To the west, thunder rolls, mocking the skyscrapers that in her time cropped up across the river like mushrooms. Sometimes she wonders whether they will be left to rot one day by those who now inhabit them, as all mortal people once abandoned her island. Every effort of man, she thinks, is but the scratch of a broken stick in eternal clay.

Just look! Weeds grow between floorboards of the gymnasium. Rust eats the iron hinges of boiler house doors. Long ago, her unhappy cottage rotted into the soil. Today, rats bathe in the puddles of its old depression.

She traps them sometimes for supper, which is only right, since she freed them in the first place.

"Mary," Mr. Cunningham, the medical supply clerk, once persisted, "have you seen who opened that cage?"

"He was dead, Doctor." She called them all doctor then. "Buried him, I did."

But she had not. She had concealed the rat in her apron—the apron they gave her for work in the admitting ward. Concealed him and freed him in the woods with the others.

They were white, the original pack, white as any nurse's starched uniform. Now, many generations later, their colors run from nut-brown to dull black. They have their warrens under the leaves, where the forces of nature cut fissures in the schist of the forest floor. Also, no more than a few dozen live under the warped gymnasium floorboards. There is not enough natural food to sustain more than that, and they will not venture nearer her sleeping quarters. They know enough to keep their distance from her, and she sets her traps far from where she usually rests her head.

The thunder nears. It rattles loose windowpanes in what remains of the vast hospital.

Without breaking stride, she walks through the pitch dark, accustomed to it. Even up and down stairs without touching the loose railing. Her gait is lumbering, unfeminine. Everyone always said so. It matches her guttural voice, like a mumble from the beginning of sound, from deep within the earth. Though she spoke when there were people around, few ever heard her. Now she sometimes calls into the empty rooms just to register the echo, to affirm her own tenacity.

She measures the passage of time only by the height of the choking vines, once kept at bay, now running riot. And by the changing skyline across the way.

When lightning strikes the bent rod atop the old foghorn tower, she grunts aloud, thinking maybe Mathilde will hear her—Mathilde, whose hatred burns so hot and strident. Next to it, Mary's bitterness throbs like a dull ache. No less intense, only of a different texture.

She leaves the building and walks down to the pebbly shore, follows it along as the rain starts to fall in fat drops, hissing through tree leaves.

The island has the shape of an amoeba. She traces its outline with her path, callused feet insensible to the sharp rocks and broken bits of iron and twigs and thorns.

When the lightning flashes again, she sees more ghostly forms, mostly women and children. They lie atop submerged pebbles, river water fluttering what remains of their clothing the way breeze stirs the frayed wings of a decaying moth. The sight of them no longer surprises her— not even their charred and blistered faces, their stump fingers, their pleading stone-dead eyes.

Is that water or trapped air or fistfuls of posies bulging their pockets? She may never know. They lie beyond her reach.

Ashes! Ashes! We all fall down.

Fire always factors into life's most plaintive moments, does it not? No matter whether it comes from outside or within.

And there is always blackness, too.

"Mary," calls Mathilde through the wind-driven rain. "Mary!"

"I'm here."

"This happened not by accident. Men it was did this. Men."

Mathilde harries her all the way along the path in the muddy woods and through the door and up the steps and down the hall and into the old laboratory, where she stops. Blue lightning illuminates in flashes the damp dusty room, and she sees George A. Soper standing there, imperious. Stiff like his instruments.

"Leave me alone, Mr. Soper." The only one she will not call doctor. "Leave me alone or I'll take out your eyes with this here—"

She clutches the sturdy carving fork in her fist, eighteen inches long, the tines sharpened. She had it in hand when they first pursued her, and she will never let it go.

"Now, Mary," says Soper. "By one means or another, I'll have that sample."

"You won't!" She screams and charges him. But he is gone, long dead. The points of the fork bury themselves in the wooden cabinet. Its shaft twangs, vibrating at a high frequency.

She outlived Soper—has long outlived all those who strapped her down and had their way with her.

Ring around the rosie. A pocket full of posies. Ashes! Ashes!

Yet he haunts her still.

The rain presages something. She feels it.

She squeezes a drop of water from her hair into her palm and licks what tastes like vinegar. Acid. It eats the island hardscape. The world changes but she does not. The world ages. She maintains.

Sometimes—rarely nowadays—men visit the island. Never to stay. Only to check on things or to snap pictures. She hid from them all these years, but must she forever?

The storm is passing. It leaves behind the scent of electricity and rotting fish. And a sense that something is different this time, her environment altered. No living person stands across from her in the dark laboratory, yet the man's terrible presence persists longer than it ever has. Soper.

"He's coming for me," she says aloud.

"No," whispers Mathilde into her left ear. "You are coming for him."

Karalee

KARALEE SOPER SITS on the back bench of a Boston Whaler, cruising down the East River with four of her closest friends. On Karalee's lap rests her dearest possession: a brand-new Nikon 35 mm camera that she purchased on layaway from B&H Photo on Ninth Avenue in Manhattan. The Nikon replaced a Canon that she had owned from freshman year of high school straight through college, her first 35 mm and her first love. For eight years she carried that camera everywhere, wearing through three cases and yearning for a darkroom where she could develop her own shots. She carried it so incessantly that it made her father jealous, and he would tease her about it, sometimes hide it from her, other times cover his face with his hat to ruin her shot. That camera was the first thing his eyes settled upon when she told him more than a year and a half ago that she might want to change her career plans. He threw it so hard that it exploded against the stone kitchen wall of their house in Pelham, the lens cap catching her left ear as it sailed by, cutting her.

The scar on her ear itches sometimes. It remains fresh and pink, a thin line running from the antihelix—she knows her anatomy—through the scapha to the helix. But the loss of the camera disturbs her worse than the damage to her body.

She wishes she'd had the reflexes to snatch that camera out of midair.

Instead, it shattered against the wall into thirty-nine pieces—she counted them through tears—the same number of lashes that Jesus received. Although her father apologized when the blood began flowing, the broken camera felt like that kind of loss to her at the time, like religious-scale suffering. She mourned for two weeks and acquired the new Nikon with her own money, saved from busing tables over two summers. Although she couldn't afford to buy it outright, she made the down payment with a few bucks to spare. Thirteen more months, and she'll have it paid off.

On the way downriver from Poughkeepsie, she shot an entire roll of film, mostly taking portraits of her friends, they who playfully call themselves the Sewer Rats. She is profligate with film—can't help herself—but that improves the odds of a great shot. For instance, she snapped half a dozen pictures of Chick at the helm, and one or two actually might have come out quite well. His round, red-cheeked face glowed in the early sun, his gaze falling on the Tappan Zee Bridge as they prepared to pass under it.

And she may have captured a characteristic gesture of Josh's, the way he pushes the black-framed glasses back up his nose with the knuckle of his pinky finger. But she got only one of those, and it's entirely possible she had the shutter set too slow and it blurred.

She snapped a good picture of Gerard, she thinks, in his San Diego baseball cap, reading a mass-market paperback copy of Norman Mailer's *Executioner's Song,* holding it up in front of his buff, bare, hairless chest, soft Korean eyes riveted on the words like nothing else existed in the world at that moment. Gerard, so easily distracted in other respects, focuses like a laser on printed words.

She may very well have done her best work so far with Estela, getting the Spaniard in midconversation, that flamboyant sweep of her black hair, the waving around of that half-dead arm of hers. In one unselfconscious motion—frozen in film, Karalee hopes—Estela flaunted her determination not to let anything hinder her, least of all her physical limitations.

Karalee lifts the camera to her eye again as their boat, the *Flagellum,* enters an area of the East River known as Hell Gate. But there's nothing worth noting in the frame. No one doing anything interesting, and the skyline behind them looks dull in the haze.

She feels a rumble from the boat's engine, which springs to life like an animal newly alert, and although she never held the wheel, she has a sense that the river is resisting them here. The engine's vibrations travel up through the soles of her bare feet—up through her hamstrings and the small of her back, too—and flutter her guts. Something like the feeling she knows from trips to Rye Playland, when the Dragon Coaster takes a precipitous drop, and for one fleeting second you confront your own mortality. But the river today holds no further sense of drama. It is stippled only by the tiniest waves.

Thirty minutes ago, Josh began calling out random public health facts, such as the amount of effluent that used to pour untreated into the waters around Manhattan and how yellow fever arrived from Barbados at the end of the seventeenth century. Now this casual recitation has segued into a full-blown lecture, Karalee listening with only half a mind. She looks out across the river and notes how the urban enterprise overwhelms what little bits of nature they can see. Buildings tower over trees. Bridges disrupt the sweep of the river. Planes and boats force waterbirds to the margins, where the Sewer Rats saw a few ducks and herons on the way down. Nature endures if you look hard enough. It's there if you scratch the façade of civilization.

One aspect of photography that Karalee loves most is its ability to scratch that façade, to explore the layers of people and things. Even when she can't find them with the lens—for now she returns the camera to her lap—she likes to catalog the layers in her head.

She thinks of her place as a physical object on the earth, listing in her mind that which lies beneath her now: the thin nylon, damp with sweat, of a modest navy one-piece bathing suit; a boxy pair of tan Bermuda shorts that Chick hates because they make her ass look big; in contact with those shorts the lightly soiled vinyl boat cushion with torn piping, stuffed with spun petroleum; then the hard slick fiberglass bench and hull; the striated gray water that fights the boat, struggling to wrestle them backwards and dump them into New York Harbor; finally, the hidden sheer rock cliffs of the channel, deepened by dynamite a hundred years ago to allow for the passage of ships much larger than this small pleasure boat.

What lies at the base of the underwater cliffs? Josh, when he imparted this bit of information, didn't say. He has moved his running disquisition onto the subject of Randalls and Wards Islands, which they just passed. Pot and alcohol make him garrulous. Gerard and Estela, expressionless, listen with the laughable focus of stoned people peering through mist. Maybe that's why, all at once, they've become so unphotogenic. Chick, for his part, grips the wheel with two hands and appears to have other things on his mind.

Josh speaks of how nineteenth-century New Yorkers used the East River islands as a way to banish the sick and forlorn from their sight. On Wards and Blackwell's and other islands, they built quarantine hospitals and orphanages and poorhouses and retirement homes for disfigured Civil War veterans. Later they built madhouses and prisons. They disappeared the unwanted dead there, too, even disinterring and reburying those unfortunates who moldered in Manhattan's original potter's fields. These souls would find no peace in death—no more than they had found in life. Wasn't it always this way? Uneasy rest for a man who impedes the course of progress.

"Here lies Tom, who weren't known to anyone with the scratch to afford him a proper burial." Josh giggles, putting on something between a cockney and an Appalachian accent. He's from Roslyn Harbor, a wealthy Long Island suburb, and "doesn't know from" poverty—at least not the real condition beyond the statistics that he's studied ad infinitum. "Died on the sidewalk of Canal Street," he continues, narrating the life of fictional Tom. "Buried in the earth of Madison Square. Dug up to make room for a park where the bourgeoisie could soak in the sun and sit in the shade. A fresh hole dug on some godforsaken island. An unmarked grave as anonymous as the life he once lived."

"Oh, shud up already." Estela's brash Latin accent compensates reasonably well for the vulnerabilities she can't hide. Her body may be out of balance, but her mind and her determination sing in perfect harmony.

Josh shoves his glasses back up his nose with a pinky and squints in her direction. He is gangly and scoop-chested, no more than a wisp of hair showing between his paper-plate pectorals. "Do I offend you?"

"Worse." Estela exaggerates a sigh. "You're boring me."

Since beginning his lecture about the islands, Josh has uttered few facts they don't already know. All of the Sewer Rats attend the Graduate School of Public Health at Havermeyer University—everyone but Chick, who's a junior professor. They are the best and brightest of the doctoral program, in fact, capable of citing obscure statistics and macabre bits of history, such as the geometric progression of the Black Death or the number of World War I soldiers who died from dysentery in the trenches along the Marne.

Josh blushes, adjusts his chin as if Estela has slapped him, and looks to the two other men for support. But their attention has turned elsewhere. Again: stoner focus. Karalee is the only sober one on the boat, has never touched more than the occasional glass of wine or beer, fearing it will make her sloppy. She lifts the Nikon to her eye but misses Josh's pout by a fraction of a second.

"Thar she blows!" Gerard calls, smiling proudly through squinted eyes at his own bit of inanity. He's staring at the Bronx shore; they all are now. He drops his water-stained paperback onto the copilot's seat—the copy that he's carried all summer like an old friend, visiting and revisiting it. The book bounces off the seat cushion and lands on the deck, but Gerard hardly notices. He's looking at the smoke in the sky.

Karalee follows his gaze.

Mary

SHE IS ALONE, but no more alone than she ever was.

Next morning, the halls of the old dormitory are quieter than the dust that plasters every untouched surface. Disrupting the silence, her thick bare feet clop on loose linoleum tiles almost as loudly as the blocky high-heeled brogues that she once favored. She recalls the sound they made in the tenement stairwell on Third Avenue, climbing on her rare days off to discover the empty room at the top with Briehof's doused cigarettes floating in glasses of cruddy water.

Sometimes she would wait for him to stumble in with the dog. At other times she went down again to find him at the bar across the street, surly and brooding. She would ask if he had eaten and he would nod noncommittally to his whiskey, and did she not feel alone then? But she always allowed him back into bed, the tenement room being so cold otherwise and sleep so elusive with trains rumbling night and day on the elevated tracks outside.

In the old country, in Cookstown, the only girl in a family of boys, she walked the streets in her brothers' hand-me-downs and appeared to all the world like an orphaned guttersnipe. No one ever got too close to her. Her simpleminded mother would not meet her eyes or anyone's, as if she concealed a shameful secret. Mary learned to cook not at her mother's apron strings but by observing from the corner, where she crouched many afternoons with a thick wooden splinter to pick the coal dust from beneath her fingernails. Those nails! For all her efforts, they held dirt like a starving man clings to a crust of bread.

Now being alone and unmonitored and forgotten on this island might provide the only blessing she ever had: the freedom to abandon all efforts at cleanliness. Her nails are black not just underneath but deep around the cuticles. Her teeth—a full set yet after all these years—gleam brown like snail shells. Her thick hair—still mostly dark—is matted and oily.

On hands and knees she tends her garden, rarely needing tools beyond her fingers in the well-crumbled earth that she has worked all these decades. Today, after the rain, with her skirt hiked and gathered to her waist, the soil feels cool against her upper shins. Despite the hot sun this morning, the days grow shorter and frost will soon come—the end of fresh vegetables. Already she has gathered many seeds in preparation.

A gust of wind passes through the greenery, leggy plants swaying, held erect by frames that she improvised. Something peculiar moves in the climbing peas. She looks up to see she has snared not one rabbit but a pair—an unusual bounty—swinging in the breeze. She rises and unties them.

The heads hang limp from her open palms. Their soft fur is damp with dew. She takes them into the kitchen and uses a sharp knife to gut and behead them, to strip the skin off, and to quarter what remains. Blood from their viscera drips off the butcher block and puddles on the floor. She leaves it for the flies and browns the rabbit pieces in hot oil, then using quick strokes chops up an onion, a potato, and some vegetables and tosses it all into the pot with water from a bucket and a third of a bottle of red wine. The wine is undrinkable but adequate for the base of a stew.

At the Warrens' in Oyster Bay she made rabbit stew sometimes. Like her, the banker preferred his food hearty, even in summertime. He ate with gusto and despite a houseful of servants never showed the table manners to suit his station in life. It was said that his father grew up working class in London, but she does not know. The man never spoke a word to her, nor did his wife. Mary reported to the housekeeper, who turned up her nose at the cook.

When the trouble started at that establishment, with the children upstairs melting from disease and the household in a fevered panic, Mary slunk away just as she had arrived. Alone.

Leaving the pot to simmer, she steps out and gazes through the trees toward the southwest shore. There, all those years, she had her two-room cottage—down by the lighthouse. To say she made peace with her confinement there—no. No! But there she ground on in solitude as months and years turned to decades, as the doctors and nurses and orderlies stepped lively for the last boat leaving the island for good, and well beyond that, until the cottage roof collapsed and it no longer provided proper shelter.

Now, if Mathilde's prediction is correct, her isolation might soon conclude in some fashion. But if Mathilde is so smart, why did she and both her children come to such a violent and miserable end?

On the other hand, that woman does now possess depths of knowledge learned the hardest way, in the hardest place.

Among the impotent and loveless, wisdom is its own form of purgatory.

Karalee

THEY CAME TO this part of the river for the fire. It gave purpose to their aimless pleasure cruise—the last of the summer, the last before Chick lists his boat in the pennysaver for 20 percent less than he paid. They'd just passed under the white steel latticework of the University Heights Bridge when Chick spotted what he thought were thunderheads. He was ready to turn around and retreat north to the Hudson when Estela, who interned one summer as a radio meteorologist in Barcelona, reasoned that those couldn't be normal storm clouds, and therefore must be billows of smoke from a giant fire.

No one believed her at first. Did Catalonian clouds even behave the same as New World ones? But shortly thereafter, a pair of police boats raced by with blue strobes flashing, sending Josh and Estela into fits of paranoia that almost caused Gerard to toss the marijuana overboard. Chick talked sense into everyone by observing that the cops could no more see their puffy eyes than they themselves could see the cops' faces. And besides, if the police went around arresting every wasted boater in New York, they'd have to add a new wing onto the Tombs. More interesting, there was an epic fire somewhere in the Bronx. How cool to check it out, see what they could observe from the water.

Karalee and Estela couldn't have cared less about rubbernecking a fire. "Why don't we find a beach?" Estela pleaded as they passed East Harlem and Bronx Kill. She already had the bikini on, made sexy not by her flat chest and her thin toneless legs, but rather by the aplomb with which she carried herself. "It's the last time out on the boat and pretty much the last warm days of summer. As a matter of fact, there's a cold front coming in tomorrow." She stuck out her lower lip.

But the three guys were stoked by the possibility of witnessing death and destruction firsthand. So here they are in Hell Gate, approaching the Bronx shore.

Boys and their bulldozers.

Karalee imagines Chick as a kid putting his face three inches from his yellow Tonka dump truck—the one she's seen in his family picture album—pushing it along with such determination that he plowed down everything in its path. She has a young cousin who used to wear that slack-jawed look only boys seem to get whenever they play with cars. That same slack-jawed look that also crosses Chick's face every time he gapes at her naked body.

And after that look passes, everything accelerates.

The cars crash. He grinds her into the mattress. The fire must be found.

This mad chase in pursuit of billowing smoke reminds her, too, of her father's boundless and urgent ambition, a thought she wants to shake off as soon as it occurs to her. She lifts the camera and zooms in on the horizon, but meets more grayness: lack of contrast, of layers, of nuance.

As Chick turns the boat crosswise to the current, it rocks, and Karalee's camera bounces along on her hip.

All men, she decides, are obsessed with holes. And what is a car accident or a train wreck or a fire but a hole in the fabric of social intention, the ripping open of a fresh wound. She has no interest in pictures of fires or natural disasters. Chasing fires is as stupid as those guys who chase tornadoes—the tornado being another hole, when she thinks about it.

And yet here they all are, staring northeast across the estuary at an area of warehouses they figure for Hunts Point.

It's a big conflagration for sure, black smoke shading to gray as the fire vomits ash into the hazy midday sky. At the horizon, colors flicker.

Karalee leaves the camera down. She doesn't think they could reasonably see flames at this distance, so it must be the lights of emergency boats, of which there are many. They have converged there in droves, a flotilla of gawkers and would-be heroes, and for some reason it irritates her to think of all the wasted effort. Somewhere in that borough, no doubt, or on the Lower East Side of Manhattan or somewhere else close by, a lonely person is dying painfully but quietly in an abandoned tenement. Maybe it's a young boy or an elderly woman. Maybe a cripple or a tortured soul enslaved by heroin—real human destruction, but without the drama of an explosion. No macho glory in that rescue. No world to conquer. No fire to marvel at.

No hole to bury your head in.

The faint smell of smoke makes a claim on the air. The men on the boat practically drool as they debate whether they should close in on Hunts Point. Even Estela now seems entranced by the spectacle. She hunches over a map with Gerard and Josh, plotting a course.

These days, Gerard carries himself with an admirable level of confidence that he didn't have before he came out of the closet to the rest of the Sewer Rats during an intense dinner party six months ago. He even admits to harboring puppy love for Sylvester Stallone, which Karalee finds pathetic not for its gayness but for its lack of courage. "Now that you've found yourself, what's the point lusting after the unattainable?" she has pleaded with Gerard more than once. "The guy's a movie star and he's straight."

"You don't know for a fact that he's straight," Gerard always says. "You thought I was straight until recently."

She did not. Or, to be more honest with herself, she only suspected. Layers, again. Layers.

Gerard's Stallone obsession has accomplished one thing, at least. Using the equipment in a friend's garage, he has applied himself to a weight-training regimen that leaves him rippling with muscle. Karalee, by now accustomed to seeing his sculpted back, gazes nonchalantly past his thick trapezius to the plastic-coated map. In an instant, she spots something that tightens the back of her throat: North Brother Island—a place she knows only in stories, but, oh, what stories!

She tears her attention from the map and looks past the windshield, calculating. The island lies right over the bow at no more than half a mile. It is thickly wooded and vine encrusted, but through the haze, she thinks she discerns the peak of a large building.

Mary

Now at a vigorous boil, the rabbit stew throws off pungent steam that causes Mary's eyes to water. The steam condenses on the grease-soiled kitchen tiles that line the walls; she wipes a finger across one tile and rubs her slick fingertips together, meditating over the bubbling pot.

The flies have licked up all the rabbit blood from the butcher block—or maybe the rats ventured out when she left the room.

A different smell reaches her—something burning. But she did not see the pot boil over. She lifts it up but finds no sign of fresh blackness. Goes to the nearest window. From here people once could see the river and clear across the next island to the city, but many trees have grown up to obstruct the view. Nothing burns today on her island; she can tell that much.

She works through a warren of back hallways, once used by orderlies to remove biological waste, and climbs the stairs to her attic room. From this window she can see the river, and she catches sight of smoke rising to the northeast.

That's what she smelled. Aha. But activity on the opposite shores stopped interesting her ages ago. It is as meaningless to her existence as a dust storm on Mars.

The sight of the river, however, that's another matter. She stands constantly on guard for changes in its mood. Her jailer and her protector.

From up here it appears as a pool of shiny-smooth solder with colored blocks floating upon it. Today as every day, this view once again prompts thoughts of the Warrens to invade her mind—Mr. Warren so eager to sail with his chums that he moved his whole family out of the city for the summer months.

Most mornings, after finishing her prep work for the Warren kitchen, Mary went out to sit off by the side of the house and gaze between bushes at the water of Oyster Bay. Earlier in the summer, there had not been much of a vista there from the working end of the house, but Mary took to emptying the waste from her pots near the base of a tall hibiscus bush. After a few weeks, the bush stopped flowering. Then its leaves yellowed and fell off. When it turned bare, the gardener cut it down, leaving a gap.

It was a pretty view of whitecaps and sailboats, but it could never last. All beauty in Mary's life proved fleeting.

That morning she felt the change before the news reached her. Cloris, the Warrens' youngest daughter, failed to rise with the sun as she usually did, one less voice drifting to Mary from the breakfast seating area out on the patio. When the family dispersed, foreboding took hold of the household. Mary ignored the familiar feeling, presuming she still had time. When the kitchen was clean, she emptied the basket of peas into her apron and carried two large ceramic bowls outside, one for the peas and another for the shells. They smelled of fresh-cut grass and mint as she ran a thumbnail through each pod, severing the funiculi. It might have been a moment of divine peace, but the perfection of it unsettled her. She twisted around to look over her shoulder toward the house. No one there but a feeling.

Mary popped a few raw peas into her mouth, snapping them in half with her front teeth before appreciating the sweet milky freshness. Under a hazy sky, the sallow face of the sun had glided to a new position, rays now falling on her back, making her warm. She slipped off her brogues and relished the cool grass under her stockings, then looked again over her shoulder, but still no one had appeared.

When she completed her chore, Mary brushed off her apron with the palm of her hand, placed the bowl of shucked peas atop the bowl of empty pods, and rested both bowls in her lap, looking out once more at the bay. She felt a change in the air and knew for sure. In another moment, when the screen door slammed and Mrs. Farrell came up behind her, Mary barely turned around.

"Arabella is under the weather." The housekeeper sounded stern, as always, the whole world a problem to her that ever begged for solution.

Mary slipped her shoes back on and stood, nodding to Mrs. Farrell as she proceeded to the kitchen. By the time her fifteen-minute break came, Mrs. Warren was also reported ill. By that evening, an elder daughter, Barbara, and the chauffeur failed to appear to their respective dinners. No one rallied for dessert. Mary watched the peach melba turn to soup in their bowls.

AT THE OPEN window in the North Brother bedroom, her fingertips linger on the old brass handle, much like that of the single tiny window in her garret room at the Warrens'. She squints at a wasp with dangling legs, moving capriciously, circling as it rides the air currents. She remembers the doctor coming that night, Mary standing in the dining room doorway as he passed through the foyer with long strides, clutching his black bag.

She remembers going to her room via the back stairs and packing her few things into a cloth satchel in order to be ready for the inevitable moment, when it came.

A week later, she served breakfast to three people from a family of eleven. In the kitchen, she fed five workers from a staff of fourteen, including herself. By then Arabella and Mrs. Warren lay gravely ill. Thomas, a middle son, last to acquire the disease, was rapidly slipping away. But, then again, he had always been frail.

On the day Thomas died, Mary wiped down the kitchen with a rag. When the undertaker arrived and the household devolved into hushed commotion, she took her satchel and eased herself out the side door without leaving a note. She walked with long deliberate strides from the house to the train station for the dreary ride into Manhattan.

When she reflects on it now, she resents that she never had the presence of mind to collect her final pay from the Warrens. When Soper came around asking all those questions, he did not once ask how fairly she had been treated.

And to this day they owe her.

Briehof inquired after the money first thing when she found him at the bar. She let him touch her under her skirt that night, which proved small consolation to either of them.

The wasp outside draws wider circles, changing its strategy. It arcs away for a moment but turns for the window again, flying right at Mary. Quick as a cobra, she lunges and pulls the window closed. The wasp, a moment too late, hits the glass with a ticking sound.

Karalee

PEERING AT THE upper story of the building on North Brother, Karalee perceives a flash, like the brief reflection of sunlight reflecting off a twitching mirror. She lifts her Nikon, wondering what could have thrown such a light from this island said to be abandoned. The zoom lens helps only a bit—still too great a distance. There are birds around that she can see with the naked eye. Perhaps one of them did something that briefly changed the light. Perhaps a Mylar balloon was caught in the trees, but she doesn't spot any, and wouldn't the thermals have carried it high enough to cross the river?

She decides it must come from a casement window in motion, likely swinging in the breeze. But none of the casements looks loose from what little she can see. Maybe a gust caught the window and slammed it shut in just such a way.

Or perhaps she saw nothing at all. None of the others seems to have noticed, their attention still fixated on a plan for scoping out the Bronx fire. "They probably have fireboats out there," Chick says, looking over his shoulder at the others studying the map. "If so, they won't allow us to get very close."

But Karalee can't take her eyes off the island. Anyone who knows the history—admittedly very few these days—knows that North Brother once housed a notorious prisoner but most recently hosted an ill-conceived rehab facility for young drug addicts, as if the idea of shipping such addicts to an isolated island didn't defy every public health lesson America should have learned a hundred years ago.

The island's notorious prisoner died in 1938. Thirty years later, when the rehab facility closed, the authorities finally gave up on the hospital. The island, only twenty acres and serviced by no bridge or ferry, was deemed a vestige of another age, trapped in the rushing channel known as Hell Gate. It was best left to the birds and critters, and so the authorities left it. Since the last city employee boarded the last boat out, not a soul has rested his head there overnight. Karalee read that fact not long ago in a *Life* magazine article. And some of the buildings have been disused for even longer than the intervening fourteen years.

She wonders what's to be gleaned today beyond those trees, having peered many times into grainy black-and-white pictures of the place, one in particular drifting back to her now: an isolation ward lined with beds—patients cocking their heads toward the camera as if to project themselves and their misery onto the photographer's attention. Karalee turns her own head in that manner, and her eyes lose focus past the edge of the boat. The scar on her left ear itches, and she becomes light-headed. She feels not at all herself and wonders whether it's seasickness. But there are no waves—and, besides, she's never been ill a day in her life.

Sweat beads on her brow. Of course it does, she thinks, because the air is hot and humid. But she knows there's much more here to disturb her. There is that worshipped ancestor, his relationship to this island, and the source of tension between Karalee and her father.

She recalls—as if she could forget for a second!—that when her father threw the camera at her, they were arguing over her career plans. Oh, her father—so sure about everything. "That Soper certainty," her mother calls it. And it might serve some people, Karalee is the first to admit. Her grandfather, after all, had leveraged that stubbornness into a career as a successful defense attorney. Yet for that man's son—her father—certainty always leads to financial disaster. And don't they have a garage full of Soper Soap to prove it? SOPER SOAP CLEANS CLEANEST! Will she ever escape that misbegotten slogan? Clean, it did—nearly cleaned them out of house and home. From which event Karalee's father concluded that his only child must make a safer choice than a career in the arts, which left unsaid something Karalee knew for certain: his conviction that women ought only to make safe choices. And as usual, her mother agreed.

More than a year ago, with her camera in pieces, Karalee acceded to her parents' wishes and used her biology major to obtain admittance to the Graduate School of Public Health at Havermeyer. She was following in the footsteps of famed public health advocate George A. Soper, the great-grandfather she never knew but ever heard about, the man who first came to North Brother—here in front of her—in order to deposit his quarry: the wayward cook, Mary Mallon.

The island lies within easy reach of the *Flagellum* now, no more than a quarter mile away. A flock of birds rises above the tree line and settles back down among the branches, calling to one another. Maybe it was in fact a seagull she spotted moments ago—a flash of white wing, not a man-made reflection.

In any case, she aches with sudden curiosity.

She knows the island is largely a ruin. Might she bring back some pictures to show her father, let him see for himself that he clings to a relic? And if at the same time she could make the photos beautiful, he might yet come to appreciate her unique talents.

"That's North Brother," she hears herself saying to her friends. When no one responds, she leans over Gerard's broad shoulders and plants the tip of an index finger on the map. Louder she says, "North Brother, where they isolated Typhoid Mary. Wouldn't it be interesting to go there instead of chasing some stupid fire? It's right in front of us. There." She straightens up and points across the water.

"Typhoid Mary," Gerard says. "I forget sometimes she operated in this area. I always think of her as a person from another part of the world."

"She was Irish originally. But an immigrant to America. She spent more than a third of her life on that island. My great-grandfather, George, tracked her down and put her away."

"Tracked her like a dog," Chick says, almost with glee.

"She died there," says Karalee. "Unattached. Childless."

Estela rakes her gaze over the trees and what little she can see of the buildings. "Is she buried there?"

Karalee firms her chin. "She's interred at Saint Raymond's Cemetery in the Bronx. They say only a couple of people attended the funeral."

"Afraid to catch something?" Josh asks.

"No. Just her only friends, I guess. One other patient . . . the priest . . . a couple of nurses who worked there."

Estela nods, the left corner of her mouth curling up. "Yes, more interesting than some crazy fire," she agrees.

Karalee is happy to have an ally. Her friend, who began on hands and knees over the map, now struggles to her feet. The dead right arm, a birth defect, has an accompanying right leg in the same condition. As a result, both limbs hang awkwardly and get dragged along by the larger working muscles, manifesting as a twitch when she is in motion. Gerard offers a hand and she takes it. "We're students in public health, after all," says Estela, sucking a breath. "And her case is iconic."

Gerard turns to Chick. "Interesting. Can we land there, Captain?"

Chick studies the landscape, assessing. "The dock is shot." Nothing remains but rotting remnants of wooden pylons, extending like an archipelago into the river. "We could try directly for shore."

"But the place is off-limits to the public," Josh protests. "Could be it's a biological hazard."

"Nonsense, man." Chick is a broad-shouldered bear with furry arms and knuckles and kinky shoulder-length hair gathered into a ponytail. He throttles down the motor, but keeps one hand on the wheel, the bow still knifing into the current. He twists around, his eyes meeting Karalee's, and turns to Josh. "Who do you suppose enforces that public restriction?"

Josh picks up the map and folds it sloppily. He snaps and waves it. "How would I know? The United States Coast Guard? The NYPD? Whoever does, it's clearly off-limits. Even marked on the map that way. It's a bird sanctuary."

Karalee wonders whether she's leading them into an argument. They've had a great summer together, light class loads, plenty of room for fun. Why ruin it to prove something to her dad? But before she can offer to withdraw her suggestion, Gerard smirks at Josh and says, "The enforcers of the rules are all at the fire, Mr. Adventure." He stoops to retrieve his paperback book from the floor, fumbles and drops it, picks it up again.

"Gary Gilmore." Josh flicks a finger at Gerard's book. "That's what happens to people who don't follow rules in America."

"What? Shot through the heart for trespassing?" Chick laughs.

"Dude, Gary Gilmore murdered people," Gerard says. "They didn't get him for a misdemeanor."

"Maybe he was the last man killed by firing squad, but that doesn't mean he'll be the last person to be killed by the system," Josh says.

"Are you serious? Grow a pair," Chick suggests, brushing his pony-tail off his shoulder.

He's always been more of a risk taker than Josh, who in Chick's position wouldn't sleep with a student if she were the last woman on earth. "The worst that happens . . . they escort us off the island with a warning. Besides, they've got their hands full today. Out there." He points with two fingers. "That fire's just as bad as it was an hour ago."

"We don't know that. It's all smoke."

"Stop being such a pussy, Josh." This from Estela. "You didn't have cancer in med school and you won't get shot for trespassing on an island that belongs to the City of New York."

She's referring to the hypochondria that caused him to abandon medical school. Most first-year medical students begin to think they have half the ailments they're studying, but then the feeling passes and they return to their senses. Not Josh, who spent two miserable years convinced of his imminent demise before dropping out.

He swallows hard. "It was real. A lipoma. They couldn't be sure it was benign until they took it out."

"Took it out?" Estela will never allow Josh to save face. Probably, Kara-lee surmises, because she's secretly in love with him. "They aspirated the tumor, Josh, didn't even have to cut you open. Everyone has those fatty tumors. Want me to show you mine?"

Josh clams up and blushes. He'd probably love for her to show him what she's hiding under that skimpy bathing suit, but not in front of others.

Gerard says, "You're not talking about those mosquito bites on your chest, are you, Estela?"

She smiles, easy to tease, in her forwardness even joking about her arm and leg on occasion. She passes up further engagement with Gerard and pats Josh on the wrist. "Can't you see that Karalee really wants to go?"

Karalee thinks of her father and the anger it takes to throw a heavy object at your daughter's head, let alone using as ammunition the very thing he knew to be her favorite and most valued possession. At once she sees him in her mind's eye, standing in their Pelham kitchen, his spectacles askew, his red face resisting self-examination or contrition. When she was a girl, he hit her mother in that kitchen at least twice that she can recall, maybe three times, maybe others. She hasn't thought of that for a long time—has put it out of her mind since high school. When she did think of those moments, they were challenges to be struggled through, not analyzed, so she never attempted to understand the specifics of her parents' disagreements. Just a feature of childhood, albeit a terrifying feature that erupted on an irregular basis as if from nowhere and then subsided as quickly as it arrived.

Now, suddenly, looking down at the cooler full of beer, it occurs to her that her father must have been drunk each time he hit her mother. He took a few pops of booze each day without much effect, but once in a while he tipped past the point of no return. In such circumstances, his stubborn streak transformed into a violent one, especially if he perceived that his wife intended to defy his wishes. Karalee, if she'd been older, might have more thoroughly documented the damage.

She picks up her camera again—the new camera. It is better technically than the Canon ever was, but no more loved in her mind. She lifts it to her eye and uses the backs of her friends' heads to frame the peak of the dilapidated hospital building that pokes up from the treetops on the island. There is no way to achieve clarity on the entire field of vision, so she lets their heads go blurry and draws sharp focus on the gable of the tall brick Victorian building in the distance, where she thinks she saw the flash.

It requires little effort for her to imagine that the peak points the way forward. Like an arrow.

Taking up his friends' challenge and that of the river, Chick steers the *Flagellum* hard to port, circling the island clockwise, his intense beetle-brown eyes studying the water's surface for flotsam. A summer spent largely outdoors has bleached his thick long hair with mahogany streaks. He didn't shave this morning, and velvety stubble already casts a shadow across his round weathered face. Karalee, who harbors something close to an obsession with cleanliness, wishes he wouldn't ever go without shaving. She also wishes he would cut his hair, but he won't be swayed.

They're close enough to see real detail on the island for the first time, at first just the wooded shore, but then it opens up. On the west side, a brick industrial building hulks near the splintered remains of the old dock. Two giant chimneys, higher than the tallest trees, still stand so tall and proud that Karalee finds it hard to imagine they no longer have a role to play in this world.

After some consultation, Chick decides to steer hard for that building, thinking the current will force them past it and deposit them on the small beach just south of there. But as the *Flagellum's* bow closes in, the current carries them nowhere near, pushing them sideways back out to the middle of the waterway.

"Wicked resistance in this section of the river," Chick says half to himself. "That's why they call it Hell Gate just south of here. It's one thing in open water, quite another when you're trying to land a small craft."

"Maybe quit while we're behind?" Josh suggests.

"Nah. I'm learning. I think I'll give it another go."

Chick swings the boat around again and throttles up. Wind generated by their motion courses through everyone's hair, and Gerard's San Diego Padres baseball cap goes careening overboard, end over end. He moves to grab for it, but it settles with a small splash into the river. "Hold it!" he shouts over the roar of the engine.

The cap floats upside down. Chick reduces the throttle and takes a starboard turn with Gerard leaning out, Josh bracing his other arm. Gerard's fingertips graze along the water and catch the bill of the cap, but his touch seals the cap's fate. It spins once and goes under, disappearing.

"Capsized!" Gerard says, playing good sport. "Oh, well."

They share a laugh over it; then Chick turns his attention back to the landing, his jaw set, more determined than ever. He's a bull when he gets a goal within sight, and Karalee has seen him achieve the seemingly impossible through sheer pigheadedness—academically, professionally, and elsewhere. He got her into the sack on the third try, even though it felt all wrong to her at the time, round-shouldered Chick physically built the exact opposite of what usually attracts her. Now, at the end of summer, he's more familiar to her but probably no more appropriate as a boyfriend, violating Havermeyer's ethics code. Given the air of irrepressibility he cultivates, she knows he hates to lose this assault on the island with everyone watching, feels his manhood at stake. Without another word, he swings the boat in a wide arc with the throttle open as far as he'll dare, the hull up out of the water riding one edge, all those aboard tipping themselves against the force of it.

When he flattens out and guns for the big building, planning to run it dead on at the risk of catching a hidden pylon, Karalee's gut clutches. *He'll kill us*, they all sense for a brief second. But he doesn't hit anything, although again the river refuses to cooperate. The current pushes the little boat sideways and tosses them out again into the middle.

She sees Chick's tanned and furry arms trembling, no doubt fatigued from wrestling the wheel. He lets out a cry. "Hoo-ah!" Intones in mock voice-over: "It's like fighting the invisible force fields of a *Star Trek* episode." He's scared, trying to make light, Karalee thinks—or is he overselling the challenge just to build himself up?

Feeling the strength of the water, Karalee imagines the sheer underwater cliffs that camber to the bottom of Hell Gate. For sure, the currents here don't quite derive from nature. The engineers made a trade-off when they dynamited these channels. In any case, the island opposes an approach from this side, at least by a boat like this one, with so little ballast.

"Isn't this fun," Estela says, exhilarated. "Like the log flume, only more real. My mother never let me go to amusement parks."

"My mother *made* me go," Josh says. "I hated it."

Karalee fights a frown, knowing she must look disappointed. Gerard, staring right at her, says, "Let's try to land this thing one more time, Chick."

But Chick tells them he won't dare. With the slightest unexpected shift in direction by the current, any approach more oblique than the one he just took might crash them into the remains of the dock. Karalee thinks of Gerard's cap, upside down in the water, carried out of sight. Estela, in particular, for all her bravado, won't fare well if they have an accident of that kind. And even the strongest among them, pitched over-board, might easily get swept away by the force of the river.

They have no life vests, and the water has a will of its own. It doesn't want them to land here.

Karalee sidles up to Chick and puts an arm around his waist. "It was just a thought. I can live without this."

"But you had your heart set, Kiki. I can see it in your eyes. There must be a way onto this damn island."

"You're going to need a bigger boat," Gerard says, laughing at his own jokey reference. They rented *Jaws* just the other night, flopped on couches and beanbag chairs, smoking grass and barking out the best lines before the actors got to them.

"The hell I will," Chick says, shrugging Karalee off. "We'll just go around to the other side."

"But the cops," Josh says. "That's the side facing all the action."

Chick ignores him, just steers. He looks long and hard at Karalee, his eyes saying, *This is what my woman wants, and I'm a man who delivers.*

In spite of herself, she makes no effort to redirect him. There are so many things drawing her to this island that she can't catalog them all in her own mind. She wants to see the former isolation wards in living color, three dimensional. She wants to step into a bit of the history she's study-ing and document what's left with her own camera. She wants to resist the father trying to impose his will upon her and to connect with the great-grandfather she never met, the famous George A. Soper.

They have almost completely circled the island. As their course along the northernmost bulge carries them again within sight of the conflagration near Hunts Point and closer to it, they snap their heads around and look eastward. Near the confluence of the Bronx River, dozens of boats cluster like herd animals. Thick smoke still rises from the fire, but it's hard to grasp what the rescue boats and working craft can achieve. They look like children's toys under a cataclysmic shadow.

ON THE EAST side of North Brother, an old seawall defends the shore from the unyielding river, which has already won part of this struggle, breaching the concrete in a number of places.

Karalee zooms in with her camera and snaps a quick picture, but doubts she captured anything interesting. She observes as Chick considers the seawall, its presence indicating that the prevailing current comes from this direction. Rather than drive them off, as it did on the other side, the river here encourages them toward the island. Rising to the invitation, Chick guides the boat closer, searching for an opening in the structure that doesn't look too dangerous. But the current pushes with such force in this direction that it scares him. He turns the wheel sharply to starboard, throttles up, and pulls away. Not that he's giving up. In a moment, he swings the boat in a wide arc and makes once again for shore.

The boat comes around, and Chick finally succeeds in finding the right approach. The river has seized his stern and they're on a straight line for a significant break in the seawall. Eyes fixed on that goal, he throttles down and turns the wheel hard to starboard again.

This time the current shoves them in a perfect line, one that will carry them between two shattered blocks of concrete with rusty rebar sticking out like wild hairs.

At once they are twenty yards from shore, but Karalee senses a sudden loss of control, their approach feeling too fast to land them safely. She must be right because Chick quickly reverses throttle to fight it, and when that has too little effect, he reverses harder, the engine roaring. Large stones and smaller rocks and broken concrete lie about the riverbed in front of them, along with assorted flotsam: splintered wood and disintegrating plastic and treadless car tires.

Many of the obstacles are sharp, and clearly Chick has little command of the *Flagellum*. He might easily dash her upon the broken seawall, and then they'd all be in real trouble. But he has passed the point of no return, nothing to do but work the throttle and steer like his life depended upon it, riding out the current into the shore.

When at last Chick eases up, the river fully takes over the boat like wind seizing a kite. There's a terrific scraping sound as they surge into the rocky shore, lurching to a sudden stop, everyone thrown forward. Gerard goes down hard. Josh and Estela, grabbing at one another for support, end up in a tangle of limbs. Even Chick, with a hold of the wheel, nearly takes out a tooth.

But Karalee perceives all that as if in a dream. Feeling the surge under her, she attempts to sit back on a large cooler stuffed with pints of Häagen-Dazs vanilla ice cream and hot dogs intended for a wiener roast. The cooler lid, made slick from a coating of condensation, offers little purchase, and when she compensates for the inertia that throws everyone forward, she ends up pitching over backwards, clocking herself in the head.

Her eyes roll back. The sound of the engine and the voices and the pain in the rear of her skull all fade out at once, leaving only the sensation of a sideways drift. Then she plunges into blackness, like a rock falling down a well.

SHE JERKS AWAKE, claws of harsh vapor shooting up her nostrils and making her eyes water. By reflex, she slaps Chick's hand away from her face, sending a small canister flying.

Then she identifies the sharp odor. Smelling salts. Ammonium car-
bonate.

"Well, that's gone forever," Chick says, looking overboard. "I suppose
we got our use from it."

The other Sewer Rats surround her on the suddenly still boat, but
all she can focus on is Chick's jowly countenance. Then her eyes roll back
again and she sees her bespectacled father. He stares at her through bars
of some kind, his face twisted in irate satisfaction. It's a familiar sight,
as she has been seeing it in dreams of late—nightmares where she shrieks
for dear life until swimming up to consciousness with Chick shaking
her awake. She fears her father in these dreams, but can't get a handle on
why. Over her shoulder across the room, her trembling mother, unkempt
thicket of coffee-colored hair, frowzy in a tattered housedress, kneads
her own hands and weeps, making no effort to step forward and inter-
vene.

In the dream, as in life, it is her father who rules the situation. Karalee puts three tiny fingers through a gap between bars and he touches
them gently, with the suggestion of genuine affection.

"Oh, Kiki," he says, his expression transforming from anger to pain.
"If only you would cooperate."

But she doesn't know how. He lets go her tiny fingers and growls like
a predator and reaches to the air around her, and the earth rattles with
violence, a quake that shakes every cell in her body down to the viscera.
He is himself a force of nature. Her mother whimpers as Karalee screams
for it to stop.

And she awakens completely, smell of ammonia lingering in her nostrils. The diffuse brightness of summer sky hurts her tearing eyes.

She sits up and shoves Chick away. Gerard and Josh and Estela hover
over her, and she clambers to her feet and pushes through them, reaches
a hand for the back of the cushioned pilot's seat to steady her dizziness.

For another long moment, she can't place herself, though she knows
her friends well enough. She sees the first aid kit lying open on the dashboard shelf, materials strewn about, a sign that someone dug through it
with urgency. Their possessions lie in a heap behind the pilot's chair, the

two coolers they brought—hers with the food and the other with the beer—thrown together but intact.

Now that the crisis has passed, it's time for tongues to sharpen. "Nice soft touchdown, Skipper," Estela gibes.

"On the bright side, you cleared my sinuses for a week," Gerard says.

Josh studies the deck. "You think she's all right?" He means the boat.

"The *Fledge?* She's fine," Chick says. "The Boston Whaler is a warhorse." He grabs the anchor and throws it overboard onto the edge of the bank before tying the line to a cleat.

"What's that for?" Gerard asks.

"In case a tsunami comes," Chick says irritably. "The next Krakatoa. Did that affect your people back in the Orient?"

Gerard makes a face like, *What the fuck?*

Karalee, who feels most responsible for Chick's behavior on account of their relationship, tells Gerard to forget about it. Just Chick being Chick. And, after all, he did get them to the island in one piece.

The boat rests aground in two feet of water. Chick appears to notice for the first time that the engine is still idling away. He reaches around Karalee to turn the key, and in the ensuing quiet asks, "You really all right?"

"Never better." She touches the bruise at the back of her skull and examines her fingertips, but sees no blood. The head doesn't hurt much, but she still feels foggy, remembers the dream, almost expects to find her father among them, standing on deck. Then comes a horrifying realization: "My camera!"

They find it under a wayward seat cushion. Fortunately, she'd stowed it back in its case minutes before Chick gunned it for shore. She feels the padded case for signs of damage, then opens it and caresses the camera body. Next she lifts the viewfinder to her eye and selects the nearest tree trunk, bringing it into focus. The woods have a misty quality. For a moment, she thinks she espies people standing there and twists the lens to focus beyond the tree, but then she sees nothing but murkiness. She pulls the camera down and peers between tree trunks, biting her lip. There's nothing there. And no picture worth taking.

Gerard gazes back at where they came from. "We lucked out," he says. "This spot doesn't only shelter us behind the seawall. Also, from out there, no one can see that we beached on the island."

Chick pulls the key from the ignition. He explains that they'll all have to pitch in eventually to turn the boat around in these close quarters. Karalee, coming more fully to her senses, supposes that Estela would take the wheel in that case, can hardly be expected to apply brute force to anything, not that she'd ever admit as much. But no point in raising the issue at this moment. They can just as easily turn the boat later as now, so they decide to wait, recover from the shake-up.

After a few deep breaths, Karalee does feel her strength surging back. She doesn't know for sure how the others feel, but the adrenaline rush of their crash landing seems to have forced sobriety upon them, their enthusiasm for adventure flagging. Yet no one wants to engage the river again just now, either. Josh pops open a can of Budweiser and takes a sip with a trembling hand.

Inspired, Chick and Gerard dig through the cooler and produce their own.

"Tastes great!" Chick says.

"Less filling!" everyone echoes, even though they have the brand wrong.

Gerard offers both women a beer, but they shake their heads.

Karalee is first to leave the boat, helped down by Chick and Josh. Then Gerard goes over the side. Next Josh. They all help Estela off, and Chick follows after raising the propeller out of the water with a motorized switch. Grainy mud drips off the blades, which have a few scrapes but appear to remain functional.

Ankle-deep in the river, Karalee finds the water colder than expected but not unpleasant. Between two scrubby bushes, a large spiderweb glistens in rays of sunshine. She takes a picture of the spider—long front legs poised in a stretch, plump abdomen. It's a big one. It might be the most well-fed spider in all of New York.

The shore is rocky and unwelcoming here, forest growing right down to the banks. Karalee follows Gerard onto solid ground, scrambling over a monkey puzzle of fallen limbs and branches and tree roots, penetrating the edge of a surprisingly thick forest.

It takes more than a minute for Karalee's eyes to adjust to the deep shade of the forest. And even once they do, she finds it difficult to see contrasts. Gloom sits thick among closely spaced tree trunks, as if some great force snuffed out the light of day.

Mary

THE HOUSEFLIES ARE drunk on rabbit blood, their share of Mary's good fortune. They bomb about the industrial kitchen, slamming into windows and walls as she tastes the stew with a wooden spoon, the juices dribbling down her chin.

Savory but not yet thick enough. She sets down the spoon and adjusts the flame.

The dish needs more time, and she has plenty of that.

She carries her carving fork and sharpening stone to a table in the old cafeteria. How many meals has she consumed somewhere on these premises? She cannot recall, but she sees herself sitting for the first meal like it was yesterday—alone in the crowded hall of the Smallpox Hospital—on her plate a pile of bland baked beans and a heel of dry gritty brown bread the color of dung.

Yes, indeed. Those were the first things that passed her lips after they came for her the third time—at the Robinsons' on Park Avenue. But it is the first visit of Soper that she thinks of now as she runs the stone over the two tines of the carving fork, feels through her finger joints the resistance of each rough grain of the sharpener as it hones and polishes.

A pall had fallen over the household on account of the condition of the maid Josette and the Robinsons' beautiful grown daughter, Samantha. As she had at the Warrens', Mary kept a fully packed bag waiting in her small room off the kitchen, knowing retreat would prove inevitable. But this time she held out hope to last through the next paycheck, which she needed desperately. Briehof, too, was ill at that moment. Nothing like the illness that haunted Mary—or, more accurately, haunted those whom she touched—just a spot of the grippe. It had put him on his back, however, so he couldn't pursue the occasional day labor that kept him in booze and cigarettes and, if he had any money left over, helped pay the weekly rent on their tenement rooms on Third Avenue.

She sees herself standing at the butcher block counter, minding her business, turning pieces of lamb in her favorite marinade with her favorite tool, the big carving fork, when the houseboy came inside with news that a man waited at the front door. He handed her a note hastily scrawled on Health Department stationery. She had enough trouble reading proper lettering as it was, and she dared not share her private business with the houseboy, but she managed to figure out the gist of the note. A calling card came attached, from one George A. Soper, sanitation engineer. He wished to speak with her at once.

Mary had an idea what this could be about. Rumors had reached her of an imperious man poking around in her affairs, visiting her previous employers in the name of his grand ideals. He planned to make himself famous at her expense. To hell with those plans! She had no intention of speaking with him, but before she could object, he talked his way inside and strode through the kitchen door.

He was a balding man with a narrow face and eyes that pierced their subject from under a prominent brow ridge. He wore a thick mustache and carried his head on a stiff neck cinched with a starched collar. She detested him on sight and, if possible, detested him more when he opened his priggish mouth to speak to her. More still when she heard the million-dollar words that spewed forth.

He asked to sit down, but she waved him off, with Mrs. Holcomb, the pinch-faced housekeeper, looking on. Then he launched right into his accusations, saying he had traced no fewer than six outbreaks of typhoid fever to her hand and that she further implicated herself in each instance by fleeing into the night. This here at the Robinsons' would be the seventh outbreak.

"But I'm still here." Mary refused to cower. "As a matter of fact, they been kind to me, the Robinsons."

"Their kindness does nothing to absolve the harm that you have instigated and the danger that remains, miss."

She set her jaw and shook her head vigorously. What did he take her for? Why, she never had typhoid fever in her life, not even as a child. She had not harmed those people. It had all been a terrible coincidence.

But a shudder of dread undulated through her middle even as she protested. For she knew the bigger truth. She had watched them crawl toward death with fateful persistence—not everyone, but enough of those whom she touched—their torment beginning with a headache and cough, sometimes a bloody nose. Then came the delirium and the rash of telltale rosy spots on the chest. Finally, the excruciating abdominal pain and intestinal hemorrhaging. It was a great random culling of the humanity around her. Some never fell ill. Some suffered and survived. Others passed from this world. Nature at work in its mysterious ways.

God sorts them out; that is what she had learned in church.

Ashes to ashes.

Despite what the priests said about faith and grace, the first cases that she saw back in Ireland disturbed her, and when she saw them in those households where she had come to work in New York—where she had come to make a fresh start, to escape the ugliness of her upbringing—they disgusted her. Then they disconcerted her. She could not miss the furtive looks that came eventually, the suspicions, as if Mary's very presence imposed a blight on the household—Mary who only aimed to please with her cooking, to see them relish each morsel. And finally the cases angered her. The injustice—that this hidden plague should stand in the way of her betterment! How dare the heavens in this way challenge her right to live in peace? How dare they attempt to crush the hope out of her? How dare they!

To see the way this man regarded her, speaking of unseen tiny creatures and human excrement and asking after her most intimate habits of hygiene! His icy blue gaze raked over her, taking in her fingernails and her hands and her apron and her dress. His examination would go right up her thighs to her bottom if she would let him have a look—damn the fact that others stood watching!—right up to the parts that she did not allow even Briehof to see with the lights lit, not even at their most inebriated or intimate.

As Soper undressed her with his eyes, she shivered, tingles running where they should not go, her ears on fire, her neck flushing.

Then the man, still viewing her as if she sat at the bottom of a petri dish, said that which she would never have imagined hearing from a stranger. He wanted her to give over samples of her urine and feces and blood. Insisted upon it. The good of the household . . . of New York . . . of America . . . of the World depended upon her doing so, he said. But what of the good of Mary Mallon, whose only means of supporting herself lay here in front of her, inside this kitchen and others like it? Mary Mallon, who never raised her hand to a fly, though she was mighty tempted now to rid herself of this pest who stood before her.

He asked how she cleaned herself when she bathed and how she washed up after using the bathroom and how she attended to necessary womanly needs at her time of the month. Mrs. Holcomb's jaw fell open at that last one, and she left the room with a hand covering her mouth.

Mary did not answer these questions. She forced her attention to the vegetables she had been chopping, the sack of sugar, the lamb shoulder in its marinade. Her cleaver lay out of reach on the counter across the room, but she had her carving fork at hand.

"Miss Mallon, if you will," Soper said, smoothing his mustache with thumb and forefinger. "All this requires is a visit to the Willard Parker Hospital on East Sixteenth Street. We'll take the samples there."

Her lips went dry. "You'll take them?"

"We will draw the blood, miss, yes. You can give over the urine and stools on your own, if you like."

She pictured him hovering on the other side of some hospital curtain, letting his imagination run wild as she touched herself. At the thought of it, she unleashed a string of curses that startled him, made his head bobble.

"You do not own me!" she screamed. "Nor anything what's come out of me!"

She grabbed the carving fork in her fist and raised it, and he turned and ran, the coward. Out the kitchen door, up the stairs, through the parlor, and out onto the street. She took no pleasure in his departure. Would rather have buried her fork in the back of his throat when he opened his prim mouth.

That fork—she still has it, the very one. She continues to sharpen it, the key to its effectiveness lying not only in the point of the tines but also in the razor's edge she sharpens into them. She touches one with a thumb and almost nicks herself. Nearly there. Only when her callused finger yields a stinging cut will the sharpening be complete.

But what is this distraction? Someone has entered the room. She looks up to see Mathilde sitting in a cafeteria chair. Her hair has burned off but for a clump or two, and her skull is a weeping bubbly blister.

"We can't go blaming the spirits for our predicament." She pauses, seeming to reflect. "Men it was did this, not ghosts."

Mary wonders, not for the first time, if heat of fire or insidiousness of water issued the final blow to Mathilde and her children. She dares not ask.

"My own brother was a good-for-nothing. *Ein Nichtsnutz. Ein Faulenzer.* A layabout."

"I loved him in my own way," Mary says. He provided her a warm body if nothing else.

"He died of a broken heart when they took you away. But not for you. He missed the money you gave him for drink."

"The more he consumed, the more he felt the pain of life without the bottle."

"That was his church. A very small chapel indeed." Mathilde makes a show of looking around, as if she has not inspected every corner of the premises ten thousand times. "This island is no place for the living."

"So what would you have me do, Mathilde?" Intolerable woman.

Mary receives only a wan smile in reply. A pause from Mathilde's hectoring at least. With grim satisfaction she returns to her sharpening.

Karalee

"COOL," GERARD SAYS, ducking under a thick twisted vine. "The forest primeval."

"Not precisely," Estela corrects him. "This was all cleared once. It's secondary growth."

"Whatever."

The Sewer Rats spend their winters at desks and chalkboards, their summers on boats and beaches and in movie theaters and libraries. They are unaccustomed to woods and now find themselves wearing only flip-flops, canvas sneakers, and boat shoes without socks. But they ignore these limitations and strike out, picking their way among the trees.

Gerard has tripped twice already on sticks and roots, scraping his shins. Estela's exaggerated high step proves an asset so far, along with the care she's accustomed to taking. With his Sperry Top-Siders, Chick toes fallen leaves, looking for salamanders. They pull spiderwebs from their hair and eyebrows.

Karalee shudders, struggling against a freak-out. Bugs and fragments of leaf litter cling to all of them. Her legs feel itchy. "Estela, do me a favor."

"What?"

"Is there anything crawling on me?"

"Let's see."

Karalee spins around and Estela runs a hand over her back and the backs of her legs, brushing her off with vigor. Estela left the boat wearing only a bikini top from the waist up, and doesn't seem to mind how exposed she is. But she knows that Karalee suffers from a touch of obsessive-compulsive disorder, and that her obsession relates to cleanliness.

"Nothing there. All set."

Josh crinkles his nose. "It smells of rot out here."

"Maybe there's a graveyard," Gerard suggests.

"You don't smell rot in a graveyard. Not without digging for it."

"Regardless, when this was a smallpox hospital, how do you suppose they disposed of those who didn't make it?"

"Buried them on the mainland," Josh speculates. "Buried them in the potter's field on Wards, if there was no one to pay for a headstone."

"There's no room for a cemetery here," says Karalee, attaching her camera flash and snapping a few pictures of bright-orange fungal formations.

"You're the expert," Estela says as she waves a cloud of midges away.

"Not really," Karalee replies, shooting a picture of some interesting moss. "I have no special knowledge of North Brother."

"C'mon!" Gerard says. "This has to be like a homecoming for you."

"Can we stop this? Any connection I have to this island is a historical accident. You guys almost sound like my father." She lowers her voice an octave. " 'Greatness runs in families.' "

"Who said anything about greatness?" Gerard teases.

"Exactly," Karalee says. "Last time I checked, my father was coming out of his second bankruptcy." She thinks immediately of her camera connecting with the wall: strange wastefulness from a man who claims such wonderful self-discipline.

"Hey, look at this!" Chick calls from up ahead.

He has come upon a small clearing with green tufts of wild grass growing in clumps. There are splinters of wood about, and in the center the remains of an old tree with the head of an ax fixed in the stump. He wraps his hands around the shaft and pulls the ax out. He circles until he's facing his friends—Karalee noting the smirk on his lips, the delight in making himself the center of attention: confident professor at the head of his classroom—raises the ax high and buries it deeper into the stump with a sharp crack as the others walk up.

"What do you make of it?" Josh asks him.

Chick shrugs. "Someone chopping wood."

"Duh, but who? There shouldn't be anyone here."

"Maybe a park ranger. They must visit occasionally."

"What need would a park ranger have for firewood?"

No one has an answer. They prowl around the site for a while, but don't find any further signs of recent human habitation.

With the others distracted, Karalee rests a hand on the ax handle, feeling the smoothness along its slight curve. She has never chopped wood; her parents' lot in Pelham is small. The touch transports her, and for a brief moment she imagines herself as a goddess of Minoa, her labrys slicing through air.

Startled, she lets go the ax handle and follows without thinking.

There's a path through the leaves that leads them to a one-room brick building with the roof caved in and the door off its hinges. A tree grows through rotted floorboards.

"Careful, girls," Chick says as they poke around. "There could be nails sticking up. Tetanus."

"We can take care of ourselves," Estela says. "We're not precious flowers."

Chick rests his hands on his hips and takes a step back, looking up at the low roofline of the structure. "I wonder if that's where Typhoid Mary lived. She had her own cottage here, you know."

Karalee shakes her head. "Her cottage was white clapboard with a black roof and a small porch in front. I saw a picture once."

"Sounds nice," Josh says. "And a water view to boot, I'd bet."

Karalee snorts. "Nice if you don't mind trading away your freedom."

"What, like freedom to kill people through your own selfishness?"

"Don't be a tool." She feels her neck flush. "You know it was more complicated than that."

On the other side of the brick ruin, they find the remains of a concrete curb and an old road crumbling under weeds and ailanthus trees.

"That's Chinese sumac," Estela says, touching the leaves of one of the smaller specimens. "Tree of heaven. Not very heavenly. It's an invasive, known for choking off natives."

They follow the old road in a direction where the canopy thins, more hazy overcast visible to them. Soon they have come upon the complex of buildings that they spotted from shore when they tried to land on the west side of the island. The giveaway is the smokestacks, standing tall above towering treetops.

Karalee snaps a few pictures, wondering what her father would say if he could see this place in this condition. The whole island feels like a monument to wrecked ambition, to how fleeting human accomplishment can be. Maybe it signifies something even worse than that, although she can't yet put her finger on it.

Chick comes up from behind and wraps his arms around her, pressing into the tops of her breasts. "Penny for your thoughts."

She shucks him off. "I was thinking how quickly nature reclaims what is hers when man stops beating it back."

"Heavy." He grins devilishly. "I was thinking how much fun it would be to screw in one of these abandoned buildings. You look like dynamite with a coating of sweat on your neck."

He inhales deeply and touches her hair and she slaps his hand away. "Pig!"

Sometimes she thinks she's sleeping with him only to get kicked out of school. She took a food photography class this summer at the Culinary Institute of America, but she did it all in secret, never told her parents or Chick. Lately she feels possessed of a lot of secrets. Maybe a few more than is strictly healthy.

She holds up her camera. *"Le grand fromage!"*

They all smile. "Camembert!"

That's what they always say when the camera comes out. But this time she's not shooting people. She has zoomed in on the ivy that crawls up the wall of a building over Chick's shoulder. The ivy moves. But it's only sparrows.

THE FIRST LARGE structure they approach is the one with the tallest smokestack. It has enormous iron doors with rust stains and green paint bubbling off. Gerard and Chick put their shoulders to the doors but find them immovable. Then they discover that one of the giant semicircular arched windows along the side has been smashed by a fallen tree. The tree trunk is large and obstructs entry. Gerard picks up a cinder block.

"Should we be doing this?" Josh asks.

With Chick's help, Gerard uses the cinder block to collapse several wire-reinforced windowpanes and mullions. Because of the wire, the window glass doesn't shatter. It deforms with a dull thud and then falls into pebbles. Gerard tears away the remains of the wire; then they toss the cinder block aside. Chick climbs through first.

A thick layer of industrial-strength dust coats the floor and the equipment inside, and twin steam boilers bigger than city buses stand idle in the middle of the cavernous space. On one end, the boilers have steel plates with open doors and a series of bolts that in combination remind Karalee of chunky faces, like those that appear on the Northwest Indian totem poles on display at the American Museum of Natural History. She feels the same way about these boilers as she does about the Indian artifacts: that she is witnessing something constructed in a spirit of ambition and glory that now sits at the nadir of defeat. Gaping at it feels like a violation of something sacred, but she can't take her eyes off the behemoths.

"Look," Chick says. He pulls a chunk of coal from the debris in a scuttle the size of a one-car garage. "That giant crumbling pier we saw . . . it was built that big so the coal boats could dock. The coal fed the boilers. Steam from the boilers passed through underground heating tunnels that supplied all the buildings. Life—or comfort, at least—depended on these boilers."

They all twist their heads around. You can imagine the bustle of the place if you squint your eyes, men with shovels and blackened faces endlessly feeding the big maws of the giant machines. Karalee wonders whether the workers came from elsewhere or were drawn from among the heartier hospital patients. If the latter, it would have been a kind of slave labor. No one landed at an isolation hospital entirely of his own free will. At best the patients yielded to social pressure. At worst they were prisoners until they healed—if they healed.

A hot flash courses from Karalee's chest to her cheeks, and she searches the faces of her friends to see whether they feel anything similar. There is no sign that they do. The air is warm and still, but has not changed dramatically. It dawns on her that she feels the same way she does when the nightmares arrive. But she is awake. She knows she is.

"Kudos to Karalee," Chick says. "This place is better than a warehouse fire any day. Living history—only dead." He sweeps a finger across the cold boiler and comes up with a coating of dust, looks comically aghast, wipes it on his shorts. Estela giggles. Inappropriately, Karalee thinks. The filth grosses her out, but something more than that unsettles her. Sadness prevails here, as if everyone who passed through left a remnant of their sorrows behind. It weighs on Karalee as they exit the boiler house through a door that was hidden by bushes.

They move along. The laundry house, the maintenance shed, the worker dormitories, random crumbling buildings whose past use they can only guess at—all carry the miasma of ruined lives. The gang strolls from building to building, from room to room, up stairwells and along hallways draped in shadows. Emptiness. Emptiness. Karalee has never felt so present anywhere, but it's the presence of an intruder. She can't help but think of a rock dropped into a still pond, wonders how their intrusion ripples out, disturbing the serenity.

"These buildings seem strangely alive. What do you suppose they want?" she asks.

"Want?" Chick scoffs, but Estela is game. "To be young again," she says.

"To have a purpose," says Josh.

"But what if they do have a purpose already . . . still, after all these years?" Karalee snaps on her lens cap. "What if their purpose is to be left alone?"

"They're inanimate objects," Chick says, having none of it. "They don't care whether we come or go."

The Sewer Rats walk north through a copse of young trees, their trunks pushed up through crumbled blacktop, and arrive at the remains of the plaza in front of the imposing Tuberculosis Pavilion. A vast horizontal building four stories high, it stretches five hundred feet from one rounded corner to the other, longer than a city block. In front, weeds crack the pavement. The half-rotten slats of wooden benches sag between concrete supports.

The pavilion atrium where they enter is remarkably well preserved, all the glass panels of the skylit ceiling intact. The panes are grimy, though, and cast cheerless light.

The group roams the halls, calling out and listening to the echoes of their own voices. Josh sings a few lines from Billy Joel, beginning, "They say that these are not the best of times. . . ."

Karalee's attention lingers on the words "that sad surrender in my lover's eyes" before Josh fades out, a little spooked by the report of his own echo. In items left behind she senses the haste with which people departed. Whole sections of the building have rotted and rusted, yet certain rooms and instruments and pieces of furniture seem ready to be reclaimed at any moment and used again, as if the last person to touch them left for only a minute and planned to return.

Gerard, seemingly oblivious to this feeling, treats the whole place as his personal jungle gym. He flings loose tiles about, tries to lift items that are too heavy for one person to handle, balances upon fallen beams. But he is clumsy. He rarely hits his target. He falls off the beams before reaching the ends. When he tries to push an old wrought-iron gurney along the floor in one of the operating theaters, a wheel comes off and it topples, screeching across the curled tiles with a sound that squirrels along the length of Karalee's spine.

Chick seems equally startled. "Dude!" he says, playfully punching Gerard in the arm. Gerard, not expecting the blow, nearly gets knocked over, and the other men have to catch him. For a moment, it's a tangle of limbs and laughter. Then the absence of sound penetrating them to the bone.

In the heavy silence, Karalee allows herself to wonder whether, on nights she wakes up screaming, she sounds like the screech from the skidding gurney.

Mary

SHE KNOWS THE sound of every living thing and every dead thing on North Brother. The drone of planes that fly high overhead and the thrum of helicopters that follow the river. The rats scurrying and rabbits chewing and squirrels scrambling. The wind blowing through ruins. Rain on broken glass. Dripping fog. The hum of pleasure boats and the rumble of barges and tugboats. The buzz of every beetle and bee and fly and wasp. The North Brother trees soughing and their leaves rustling and fluttering. The calls of crows and jays and titmice and sparrows and seagulls and the cries from the family of black-crowned night herons that lives in the cove by the boathouse.

The buildings themselves issue sounds, and not just from the ghosts that inhabit them, not just from the cries of bottomless despair that animate hundreds of women and children and a few innocent men. Sometimes she hears the heavy paint peeling, the rust scaling off iron supports, screws twisting loose, air sighing through old vents. The old metal equipment ticks with expansion and contraction when temperatures change. Sometimes structural pieces of the buildings give way to gravity, a crack followed by the crash of plaster and glass.

The sound that she just heard, however—this sound she does not know. It woke her from a deep sleep. Slowly she tries to conjure it back, to relive it so that she may make sense of it.

Metal. That is what it was. Rickety metal trembling against resistance.

She puts it together with the sound of dull banging that did not drift from another island; the hum of a small motor craft very close by, which cut out abruptly; the pop of something in the woods that she suspects did not result from a falling branch.

She sits up in her bed with the carving fork in her fist and sniffs the air.

A moist waft of rabbit stew reaches her nostrils.

She pushes herself up from the bed and rushes down to the kitchen on cat feet—not her usual clomping. Pauses to listen. There are voices. Faint but unmistakable. The voices of living people far away in another part of the pavilion.

The rabbit stew looks good and rich. She turns off the flame and covers the pot, stifling the steam.

Mathilde, living in the world of shades, may have been confused. It could be that someone comes for Mary after all.

She hides the knife she used to butcher the rabbit. Rather than stow the pot in the pantry, as she typically would, she carries it to her most secret room. A thousand men could search this island, this very building, and they would not find her hiding place. It has survived every incarnation of the pavilion. When she moved here, the doctors and nurses missed it. As did the army men who were briefly housed here, the drug addicts and delinquents, their handlers and their janitors.

She is safe here from everyone, she reminds herself. Even safe from the rats and the flies. Safe—but no! She will no longer cower. Why, the meekest ghosts have been braver than she all these years. No more! If these are new sounds, she will explore them. If they be trespassers, she will follow them.

Out in the hall, all is quiet, but the air feels different. It flutters her skirt as she moves apace, tickling the hair of her shins.

Let it.

She walks through silence.

Karalee

"WHO's GOT A match?"

Chick draws a joint from a pocket of his shorts. Gerard produces a Bic lighter.

They are lolling around in the gymnasium. Chick peeled off his T-shirt and lay it down so Karalee didn't have to sit in the dust. She keeps checking her shorts for dirt marks, forces herself to get comfortable with the few she found so far. Filth covers everything. Karalee resorts to shallow breathing. The thick dust makes for intriguing photographs, but she hates to have any contact with it at all.

Part of the gymnasium roof has caved, revealing a shard of sky. The wooden floorboards, once lacquered, are now dull and gray. Where exposed directly to weather, they lay atop one another in buckled chaos like giant stalks of mounded straw.

When the joint comes around, Gerard by habit goes to pass it to the next person without including Karalee, but she holds up a hand. She can't take much more of the inner trembling that results from her effort to suppress her OCD. Estela must be reading her mind. "Do it," she urges. "It will make you feel better. It'll take the edge off."

Karalee has seen others smoke pot a thousand times. She pinches the joint between thumb and forefinger and brings the tip to her lips with everyone watching in awe. The smoke is hot. It tickles the back of her throat, but she manages to stifle a cough. She exhales through her nostrils to prove that she did it right and repeats the process.

"Hold in the smoke this time," Chick instructs, smiling. She hates that look of triumph in his eyes, the look that says he got another domino to fall.

She passes the joint to Josh and, after he's accepted it, freezes her right hand in the air and stares at it, looking for tremors. There are none. The others, watching surreptitiously as she does this, erupt in laughter, Josh choking out smoke.

When they've sucked the joint down to a roach, Chick snuffs it and flicks it out among the buckled floorboards. Karalee senses living things in the gym, but can't spot any.

Gerard rocks his head around on a loose neck, like he's following a bouncing ball. "Wow. Do you think Typhoid Mary took her exercise in here?"

"What, like in petticoats?" Estela scoffs. "It was the teens and twenties and thirties, and she was probably raised as a strict Catholic."

"Oh, like you?" Josh says.

"Don't be a wise guise."

"That's 'wise guy.'"

Estela crinkles her nose in mock embarrassment.

Gerard brings the subject back to Mary Mallon. Collectively they draw on their study of history to piece together the early years of her life, born in 1869 to a poor family in Cookstown, Northern Ireland.

"Cookstown?" Gerard exclaims. "I didn't know that. It's too ironic. Were they all cooks, the people who lived there?"

Even though she feels a little silly herself, Karalee won't accept the humor, if that's what he intends. Maybe it's just stoner talk. "When Mary grew up there," she explains, "linen weaving and hat making were the big industries. Also, brick manufacturing." She thinks of the Victorian-revival brick architecture all around them, wonders whether Mary reluctantly felt at home here in some ways.

The young Irishwoman, already fully formed at the age of fifteen, arrived in New York either on her own initiative or following a sibling.

"There's a third possibility," Estela says. "Maybe she was fleeing someone or something."

"Most likely," says Karalee, "she was just fleeing poverty."

"The unsanitary conditions among so many of the Irish poor," Chick says. "She must've been exposed to typhoid fever back home as a kid. With all that industry in her hometown, though, I wonder why she left at all. It's not like she lived during the potato famine era. That happened earlier. By the time she came along, Cookstown had begun to thrive. Why not get a job in one of the linen factories?"

"Because it was a crappy existence," Karalee says, "toiling away in those factories that were no better than sweatshops. They treated the women as second-class citizens, too, paid them less than men."

"Probably because they were doing less skilled labor," Chick says.

"Because they wouldn't train them as they did the men," Karalee quickly retorts. "They gave them the prep work. If they wove at all, they trained them on less complicated looms than what the men got, weaving products of lesser value. So, conveniently, they never acquired the skills that the men had. And looms were placed close together, making it more dangerous work for the women."

"Wouldn't it be equally dangerous for the men?" asks Josh, the expert on danger.

Karalee shakes her head. "Those long skirts the women had to wear, they could get caught in the machinery as they walked by, yanking them into the mechanism. You could get injured, maimed for life, sometimes even killed. Maybe Mary didn't want that life. She wanted something better for herself, like all American immigrants."

Of course she did. Karalee imagines her boarding a ship in Belfast for her steerage-class journey, no doubt her stomach fluttering with excitement and trepidation. If she was lucky, she had ten pounds sterling in her pocket. If unlucky, more like ten cents. Perhaps a small sack of bread, dried sausage, and just enough ale to sustain her for the journey.

And what hopes she must have had for arrival on the other end! Plenty of Irish had made the trip before her. Many New York police were Irish. The Irish were well represented among construction workers, civil servants, and politicians. They had fraternal societies of their own. A cathedral named for Ireland's patron saint. Little could Mary predict, having arrived with no benefactors, how few prerogatives would be afforded her as a poor, uneducated Irishwoman living in New York City.

"So she goes to work as a cook?" Gerard asks.

"More likely as a washerwoman at first," says Estela. "She had to prove herself trustworthy, then look for an opening higher up the economic chain."

"Slaving over a hot stove. You call that up?" Josh guffaws.

"Yes. Up, I'm guessing," says Karalee. "Oh, yes. All your studying, and haven't you ever paused to imagine what it was like to be an uneducated single Irishwoman in turn-of-the-century New York?"

Despite the social gains made by the Irish at that time, many still looked down on them. The term "hooligan" was coined to describe the rowdiest among them—a word just coming into favor when Mary arrived. They rounded up the worst of them with paddy wagons—"Paddy" being a pejorative for the Irish.

Being a cook was probably the highest calling Mary could aspire to. And, Karalee recalls, since she consorted with a drunk—albeit a German drunk rather than an Irish one—she was the main breadwinner of her small unmarried household. The kitchen beckoned. And once she got there, she couldn't afford to give that up, probably couldn't conceive of doing so.

"She starts getting people sick," Chick says, "and when the pressure becomes too great, she splits the scene. Goes and works for another wealthy family under an alias for a while until things cool off. Gets those people sick and off she goes again."

"Poor thing," Karalee hears herself saying, picturing Mary on the run. "No friends. No one to turn to but her drunken lover. What was his name?" No one recalls.

"How do we know he was a drunk?" Gerard asks.

"My great-grandfather found him in a bar," Karalee says. "He bribed him with drink to betray Mary's whereabouts. Who else but a drunk can be bribed that way?"

Chick frowns. "Betrayed, huh? You make her sound like a victim.

Dozens of people suffered horribly because of her actions. Yet it sounds like you want to defend her."

"I do not."

"You do." Chick rolls his eyes, shakes his head—his disappointed-professor look. "It's like you haven't learned how important this case was in public health. For building awareness. For showing the danger, the irresponsible behavior of known asymptomatic carriers."

"Oh, brother! Don't give me all that ideological crap. I heard it enough from my father."

For long periods of time, the Sopers couldn't get through a family dinner without reference to the great man's accomplishments. When she was younger and simpler, Karalee thought this talk sprang from her father's admiration of his grandfather George. Now she knows better. He has attempted his whole life to trade on the name rather than make one of his own. She pictures the stacked cartons that fill their garage: Soper Soap, Soper Soap, Soper Soper Soper Soap!

She mutters the inescapable slogan. "Soper Soap Cleans Cleanest!"

No one hears her.

"And in spite of your ancestor's achievement," Chick continues, "you defend Mary as the injured party. Why? Because she's a woman?"

His tone grates on Karalee's nerves, disrupting the pleasant high she was feeling. All at once, for the first time ever, Chick reminds her of her father. They look nothing alike, but at bottom they're the same. They have to be right all the time, and in order to prove that rightness, they have to make someone else wrong. Damn the consequences. Never mind whom it hurts.

Josh breaks her reverie with a tap on the shoulder. "We should get going," he says, rising to his feet. "We have a few more buildings to explore, and it will be dark soon. Equinox tomorrow."

THEY PASS AROUND another joint as they walk. Hunger pangs begin to claw at Karalee, but there's no cure in sight for it. She swallows hard, trying to ignore her dry throat. Not like there's a working water fountain here. Not like they could go to the nearest bit of shoreline and dip a pail in the dirty river.

"So . . . wow," Estela says as the two women straggle. "I can sort of dig it, you defending Mary."

"I'm not defending her. Just trying to provide some perspective. These guys—"

"It's cool." Estela hitches along. "Because, you know, I was doing some reading not that long ago. There's this whole perspective on Mary that some historians have started to advance. Turns out there were other carriers, a couple of guys who didn't get nearly so rough treatment, only went briefly into quarantine, didn't lose their freedom for life. But Soper made an example of Mary because he could. She had no standing in society."

"Yeah, well, I'm guessing those guys didn't violently threaten my great-grandfather when he came for them." For the first time since early this morning, she thinks of the large barbecue fork that she put in the food cooler with the hot dogs. She wonders how one fends off a grown man with such a meager instrument.

"But I thought you're on her side."

"I'm not on anyone's side, Estela! Okay?"

The fresh high from the new joint has made everyone voluble again, and they can't get off the subject of Typhoid Mary. Chick explains how unusual it was in 1907 to see incidents of typhoid fever among the economic elites, who generally had the best sanitation. That was how Soper deduced Mary's role in the horrible deaths of upper-crust family members and their attendants. If the disease didn't result from unsanitary *conditions,* he reasoned, it had to originate with a person who had less-than-sanitary *habits* and the ability to expose the whole family to the disease they carried. When he learned that Mary had left the Warrens' employ rather abruptly, he thought quite rightly that he had identified the nexus.

Chick is narrating the hunt for Mary's whereabouts when they find their way into the building with the lesser smokestack. They slow their pace as it dawns on them that they've entered the old morgue and crematorium.

"Now we know," Gerard says, "why in fact there is no cemetery on the island. If you died of one of these diseases, your family didn't get the body. At best, they got the ashes."

A line of ovens with cast-iron doors is arrayed in front of them along one long wall. Josh says, "As ye sow, so shall ye reap." He knocks with his knuckles on the nearest oven door—so thick, it barely issues a thud. He makes no attempt to open it, however. "Soper was a brave man."

"Picking on a helpless woman," Estela says.

"Sure, the weaker sex," Josh snipes. "For cryin' out loud, she came after him with that giant carving fork of hers. He fled, but then he tracked her down at the tenement where she lived in sin with this German cat."

"In sin?" Karalee says. "You're a moralist now?"

"At the time, that's what they called it. Anyway, in the doorway to the tenement Soper tried again to convince her to do the right thing, and Mary threatened him with a big dog that her lover kept as a pet."

"True enough." Chick continues, "The third time he sends Sara Josephine Baker of the Health Department, along with some muscle. After hours of searching in and around the Robinson premises, they find Mary hiding in a neighboring garden."

"In the outhouse!" Josh interjects.

Karalee's thinking: *Hole in the ground. Boys and their holes.* "You're pathetic," she says, "grown men chortling over an outhouse."

"Lighten up, Karalee," Josh says. "It's just ironic, is all, her spreading the disease with her shit and such, subsequently choosing to hide in an outhouse, of all places."

"Like she had so many choices."

"She may have opted to turn herself in. You know, they let her go after a few years on North Brother, on condition she never cook for anyone again. Instead, Soper found her five years later—spreading disease in the kitchen of a maternity hospital, of all things."

"The Sloane Hospital for Women." Karalee nods, but adds defensively, "None of the patients got sickened. Only the staff."

"Twenty-five infected. And two died. What an upstanding citizen!"

"She couldn't make a living as a laundress," Karalee asserts with less conviction. Her mind feels befogged from the pot, distant from its own thoughts. Not a bad feeling, but clouding her ability to reason out where she stands. "Of course Mary Mallon made bad decisions. Of course George Soper was right to lock her away for life after her irresponsible behavior. Of course people died horrible deaths because of her actions, some robbed of life at a young age." She squeezes her eyes shut, straining to focus. "But that isn't everything. Let's be grown-ups and acknowledge that life is complicated."

A tattered monarch butterfly struggles past and settles on a vine. "Ugh," she adds, reaching for her camera. "Why should one person get to define who anyone else is?" She snaps a few pictures, all the while thinking: Doesn't her father want to mold her into someone else's image the way George Soper created an image of Mary for the entire world to see? But even if her father succeeds in defining her in some way, that won't make him right.

As they exit the crematorium, she recalls something she heard once attributed to Gandhi: What a man thinks he becomes. She wonders whether in some way George Soper thought Typhoid Mary into existence.

Karalee broods as they continue their self-guided tour, taking a turn around the old dilapidated lighthouse—its tower fallen over—and poking their heads inside a nearby boathouse, where a pair of small craft decompose in shallow water, one of them miraculously still floating but trapped behind doors to the river that have warped into barriers.

The sun hangs low in the sky. Josh checks his watch. "Now we really should get going. Only an hour or so more light."

Gerard looks down to his own wrist. "My watch! Hell. I must've dropped it somewhere."

"*C'est la vie.*" Chick shrugs. "Josh is right. We'd better get going."

"My ass," Gerard says. "That thing's an heirloom. My grandfather, on his deathbed—"

"I know. Sold you that watch. Woody Allen."

"Seriously. He did give it to me. We have to retrace our steps. My mother will kill me." An idea crosses his face. "I bet I dropped it when you punched me, Chick. In that room with the gurney." He argues that they can easily swing past the Tuberculosis Pavilion on the way back to the boat. "It'll only take a few minutes."

For all the talk of time and setting sun, they walk slowly, wanting to cling to the place, knowing they'll never have a chance to return.

"Man, I'm glad you brought your camera, Karalee," says Josh. "Who's gonna believe we were here otherwise?"

They enter the pavilion through the front door, as they did the first time, but now go straight to the room with the gurney. Sure enough, Gerard's watch rests on the floor amid dust and debris.

"See?" He stoops and picks it up, wipes it clean on his T-shirt, and clips it to his wrist. "Thanks, guys."

Chick lights another joint in celebration, forgetting the press of time, marking the third time in her life Karalee smoked, and all in a few hours. In the process, she has lost some of her inhibitions with respect to filth. She looks at the smudges on her shirt and shorts as if they exist in a different country, not here on her person. It's not the end of the world, being dirty. You can always wash it off later.

When they finish smoking, they decide to take a final twirl through the pavilion, having missed several hallways the first time through. In short order, they come to a laboratory, clothed in dust, windows facing west. Motes float in amber rays of light.

Josh depresses the old-fashioned cylindrical light switch. It clicks but no lights come on. "No electricity."

"Duhs" are said all around.

"All the more reason to get going," Josh reminds everyone.

"Chill out, brother," Chick urges. His eyes are red and swollen.

Estela hooks Josh's arm with her lame one and rubs it with her good hand to reassure him.

The lab has black stone counters, sinks, and hookups for Bunsen burners. Lining the shelves are empty beakers and pipettes and other glassware, some of it broken, all of it coated in dust.

Karalee plays with a few settings on her camera, hoping to capture the light refracting into colored gems as it passes through ancient glassware.

Gerard opens a cabinet and begins poking about. Finding little of interest, he opens another door. And another. "Hey, look at this."

He removes a black box, paint worn off at the corners, revealing the tin below. It's about six inches long in each direction, and there's an old paper tag on it, but the writing has faded. "Could be an *M*. You think this is hers?" Without waiting for an answer, he sets down the box on the island counter and lifts the latch. The box squeaks as he raises the hinged lid. There are test tubes inside, old corks stopping cloudy liquid from leaking.

"Are you insane?" Chick says. "Put that down."

"It *is* down."

"Leave it alone, dumb-ass. You don't know what's in there."

Gerard holds up his hands. "Chill out, man. It's, like, fifty years old."

"Biological agents can persist for a long time unless something comes along to kill them. If they saved that substance—"

"Okay. You're right." He folds his arms and backs away from the box. They all do.

"This is creeping me out." Josh pushes his glasses back up his nose with a pinky and presses trembling fingertips into his temples. They follow him back through the doorway, Gerard apologizing as the door swings closed behind them, not quite latching. "Can I offer some fine weed to calm the nerves? Medicinal purposes." He lights up another joint before anyone can answer, tokes twice, passes it around.

They're working their way out of the building now, but Chick can't resist poking his head through one more doorway. "There's a whole other wing this way," he observes, proceeding straight through to only mild protests.

Everyone is high again—higher than ever. Karalee has begun to see the world through a haze. She wonders whether it's the poor light or the effects of THC as she follows Chick through the remains of the old cafeteria.

On the back wall are three sets of swinging doors with round windows. One pair of doors is stuck open. They walk through those to the kitchen.

"Look at this," says Chick. "I really dig checking out the infrastructure that kept this place running, don't you?"

The kitchen is not nearly so dusty as the other rooms they've seen, maybe because the ceiling and walls are in better shape, not decaying so quickly. He lays his hand on things as he walks: the stainless steel worktables, the giant freestanding dough mixers, the butcher block, the enormous gas range. He freezes there. "Hmm. It's warm."

"Yeah, stuffy in here," Estela says.

"No. The range. Feel it." He moves his hand from one pot support to another and back. "This one."

Estela uses the backs of her fingers. She frowns, puzzled.

"You feel it?" Chick persists.

"Yeah. I guess so."

"What do you mean, you guess so?" He redirects his attention. "Karalee? Josh? You feel it?"

Karalee rests a hand on the iron spokes. The warmth, paradoxically, makes her back go clammy. She wonders if the weed is turning them paranoid. "It's faint but real. How can that be?"

Chick twists one of the stove knobs, sniffs, twists another. Karalee doesn't smell any gas. Neither do the others.

"It's impossible," Karalee says. "Must be some kind of illusion."

"An illusion of touch?"

"Maybe an inconsistency in the material causing an aberration."

"I like how you think. Beats my theory."

"What's that?"

"Ghosts."

"Shut up."

Chick laughs.

Gerard wanders off a few paces. He arrives at a solid door that appears to be in good working order. He pulls the handle and it opens. "Jackpot!"

Mary

SHE WENDS HER way through the woods with great efficiency, following no marked path but proceeding with assurance. Every so often she pauses to listen, twists around to peer between tree trunks.

The woods are alive. With life that now is. With life that once was.

The former are the rats and birds. Squirrels. Chipmunks. Slugs and flies and beetles and hidden salamanders. A few rabbits. When the island was full of people, these wild things clung to the edges in small numbers. Now they run riot, but they don't bother her.

It's the others that harry her every step, as if she were crushing their skulls underfoot. They are ghosts of the *General Slocum*, ever stirring but most active when the light changes, as it is about to do. Also when the season shifts, which insults their injury, parades before them the reminders of lost time. They wail for help, thrash from pain, rage over the injustice of what has befallen them.

She spots one or two, skittering in from the shore. Most are dripping wet from the waist down and consumed by orange flame from the waist up. Like human candles. And such they were, melting into eternal torture.

Ashes! Ashes! All fall down.

She arrives at the small clearing and sniffs. A good nose is a cook's friend. It distinguishes rawness from doneness, freshness from decay.

Will hers smell living humans recently present? She doesn't know. It has been so long. But she sniffs anyway, drinks in the scene with her eyes.

Someone passed through here, she concludes. Newly. Just today. Footprints stipple the moist soil. Leaves pile where the wind would not have carried them.

Circling her chopping stump, she thinks of the sounds she heard not two hours ago, the screeching of metal. No fool she, despite what Soper would have others believe. The health authorities. The coppers. Dr. Baker, who sat on her when they captured her the first time, holding her down with her bony rump—not much meat on that prissy witch!— while the men pinned her arms in the wagon bed as if immobilizing an animal for branding. And the judge who pronounced her sentence without listening to her side. Mr. Pulitzer and Mr. Hearst and the circulation war that they waged in complete disregard of truth and human kindness. They used her, all of them. Didn't they? No less Briehof and that useless pooch of his, eating her out of house and home. So much so that even from the grave, Mathilde could not deny the parasitic nature of her own brother.

Does she feel Mathilde here now in the woods? No. For a change, no. Let her rest; she may need her soon. But not yet. The important thing is that the woman presaged these events, prepared Mary's mind for the shift that has been a long time coming.

Mary turns her attention elsewhere, driving Mathilde from her thoughts, lest she summon her too soon. The harsh cry of metal inside the pavilion perked her ears, but it didn't end there. She found the boiler house window rudely shattered, dust disturbed here and here and here. Later, from her secret hiding place, she followed the sound of the human voices with great care. If she could sneak up on a rat in the gymnasium, she knew she could get close to any person there without making herself known. Some of the heating tunnels have collapsed, but the one that leads to the gymnasium remains wide open. Under the grates, in fact, the bend in the big cast-iron pipe magnifies sound from within quite nicely. Usually it is only *squeak squeak squeak*.

Today it was something much more.

They were only disembodied voices—she dared not scramble to the grate to look—but she is accustomed to evaluating the incomplete. Quickly she identified five people: three male and two female. They were debating who she was, Mary, doing battle to put their finger on her story. And, oh, wasn't she used to that, too? The presumption of it! It infuriates her to think of it, always has—this very attempt to mold her to their own prejudices driving her to endure when all of society has counted her out.

She thinks of what she heard as she lays a hand on the chopping stump in the woods and feels its splintery edge. The bark is chipped off there, but she did that. The ax, that's a different matter. It faces the wrong way, the handle east when she always leaves it pointing west. And she never embeds it so far down. It took some strength to do that, she thinks. *We'll see how strong he is when the time comes.*

He. Oh, yes. She feels sure it was a man who planted this ax. Only men use their strength so gratuitously.

She fondles the handle, worn smooth from all these years of work. She replaced it once herself, carving and attaching it using abandoned hand tools she found in the shop. Like all her favorite instruments, the ax, so heavily employed in solitude, by now feels like an extension of her own body.

To think someone else touched it after all this time! More violation! But how could she expect any less from a descendant of Soper and those who consort with her? Soper, yes. She heard their talk of a great-grandfather and easily inferred which voice belonged to his kin.

With fury rising in her chest, Mary pulls her skirt up over her left knee and raises her heel to the height of the chopping stump. She presses her foot down into the stump and braces herself, thinking dark thoughts. Then, wrapping callused hands tight around the handle and rocking back and forth, she pries the axhead free. She rests the handle on her shoulder, enjoying the weight of it there, and resumes walking toward the water.

Karalee

GERARD HAS FOUND the pantry. He holds up his lighter for illumination and they all pile inside. It's a large closet the size of a small room, and much to everyone's surprise, it remains stuffed with goods.

"They left it all behind," Josh says, astonished.

There are large cans of cooking oil, jars of preserves, sacks of flour, bottles of soda, tins of cookies, and enough condiments to supply a rest stop on the New Jersey Turnpike for years. They can't take inventory of it all in the dim light.

"Ow!" Gerard lets the flame go out and waves his fingers in the air. "Hot!" He waits a few seconds and strikes the lighter again.

They grab jars of pickles and large bottles of Coca-Cola and tins of no-name chocolate chip cookies and bags of potato chips with expiration dates of 1963, nineteen years ago. "Yum," Chick says in anticipation, carrying the chips out to the kitchen. "It was a very good year." He tears the bag open and begins stuffing his face. "Not bad. Maybe a little stale."

Karalee wants to be grossed out, but she yearns for food along with everyone else. She scarfs her share of sweet and salty, washes it down with gulps of Coke.

"As I always suspected." Josh belches after a long draft of Fanta orange soda. "Those expiration dates are bullshit. Why do you think they abandoned all this chow?"

"What were they going to do with it?" Chick speculates. "The hospital was closing. It probably would've cost them more to move the foodstuffs than to write them off. And this is the City government we're talking about. The bureaucrats probably sent a shipment of supplies six days before they rolled up the carpets." He chuckles. "Easy come, easy go. I bet they left propane in the tank, too."

He rests a hand on the range top again and shrugs. "Cold as the others now. Hey, Gerard. Lemme borrow that lighter for a sec." He takes it from him and twists the range knob wide open again, places an ear beside it to see whether he hears any gas coming out. He shrugs again and flicks the lighter beside the burner. Nothing.

"Don't get weird on us, Chick," Estela says, smirking.

"I'm not. It's just that . . . I could swear that was warm when we came in. You felt it. Karalee felt it, too."

"Maybe we hallucinated it," Karalee says. "I could swear I was floating on air when I came in. Now I'm down on two feet."

"Drugs wear off. That's the trick that science plays on us. Bloody metabolism."

"From the Greek for 'to change,'" Gerard reminds everyone.

They go on about words they know with Greek roots, but Karalee has stopped listening. Fingering a tin of cookies, she feels a premonition coming on, stifles flashbacks of the disturbing dreams she's been having. She steps back inside the pantry and runs a finger across the nearest box. There's much less dust than they've seen elsewhere. Then again, unlike those doors leading to the other rooms, they found this door shut tight.

Now THEY REALLY must get going. In a few more minutes, they work their way out by a rear exit of the Tuberculosis Pavilion.

The shadows have grown long outside. They estimate the shortest route back to the boat and head in that direction, which will take them past the partially collapsed greenhouse by the edge of the forest.

"How old was Mary when she died?" Estela asks.

Karalee tells her sixty-nine. Not bad for her time, especially considering the disease she carried, not to mention half a life lived in an institution. "She worked in the wards all but the last few years."

"Seems a strange place to put her, considering she was a carrier," says Estela.

"They probably monitored her hygiene," Karalee replies, "wouldn't allow her direct contact with the patients or their food."

"So she really was in a kind of incarceration here."

"I imagine so. She certainly couldn't leave the island of her own free will."

"Did your family have any private pictures of her?"

Karalee shakes her head. "Just what's in history books. There are only two or three photos that survived. Poor people couldn't afford to have photos taken, and the newspapers mostly ran cartoons that made her out to be a beast."

"She sort of was a beast, wasn't she?" Chick says.

Karalee scowls. Even bright men can be so dense at times. Can't he see that Mary Mallon was persecuted? Just a little bit at least? The very moniker Typhoid Mary imposed a degree of ostracism that no one else in her situation was subjected to.

"Of those few photos, a couple are from the early days of her confinement, when she was at her most famous—"

"Or notorious."

"Shut up already, Chick. Then there was one photo of her as an older woman. She doesn't even look like the same person."

Estela raises an eyebrow. "How so?"

Karalee thinks back to what she saw. She's been through the books a hundred times. "She looks at peace, I guess. And older, of course. The fire is out. I've thought sometimes that maybe she was like a human chameleon. Contemporaneous written descriptions of her are inconsistent, to the point where they don't all give her the same color eyes."

"That's weird," Estela says.

"I thought so, too, at first, but these Irish washerwomen and maids and cooks were all invisible to the educated class in their way. She blended into the background."

Estela finishes her thought. "Which is probably why she was so hard for Soper to catch in the first place. She was a nonentity."

"A nonentity who killed," Josh chimes in. "Remember. That's the part that made her infamous, notwithstanding your revisionist history." He straightens the glasses on his nose with a pinky and looks ahead.

Gerard and Chick are first to have reached the greenhouse. The size of a small barn, framed out in Victorian wrought iron, it's a wreck like everything else in some ways, with many glass panes missing and doors off their hinges. But in other ways, it appears to be remarkably intact. Vegetables grow in the raised beds.

Karalee snaps a picture.

Gerard snaps a ripe cherry tomato from a caged plant and pops it into his mouth.

Chick pulls his arm away when he reaches for another. "Don't eat that, dipshit."

"Why not? It's a tomato."

"It's not yours."

"It's not anyone's."

"Of course it is. Can't you see this garden is cultivated? There's not a weed around, and the soil is freshly turned."

"Was that done by ghosts, too?"

"I wish. I'm beginning to suspect there's a caretaker on this island, someone watching over it. The last thing I need is for us to get caught stealing on top of trespassing. You guys will get off with a warning, but I might lose my job."

"I—might—lose—my—job," Josh mimics. "Might've thought of that long ago, Professor."

The gibe makes Karalee squirm—a thinly veiled reference to the illicit relationship between her and Chick, something the Sewer Rats never openly discuss. For his part, Chick ignores the remark.

Gerard lets out a yawn. "I could use a nap. My sense of adventure is waning with the day." He places his hands on his hips and looks to the west. The sun has disappeared behind the trees, just a few narrow shafts of light glimmering through.

"We should really get going anyway," Josh says.

Chick agrees, reminding everyone that big boats ply the river at all hours, and even under the best of conditions, it's a long trip back to Poughkeepsie in the dark.

A GUST OF breeze rattles the woods as they trudge back to the boat, tired from their explorations. In the poor light of dusk, Gerard trips twice on branches and almost goes down hard. Josh, so focused on the way forward, nearly conks his head on a low-lying limb. Chick, assuming the role of adult, walks in the lead, urging them on. Now thinking again of his modest skippering skills, he worries aloud about how easily they'll turn around the *Flagellum* in the tight quarters behind the seawall.

Karalee walks with her arms folded across her chest, less willing to get dirty than when she was high. The cold front has finally established itself, dropping temperatures into the low sixties. Whenever the breeze blows, it sends a chill across her chest. But that's not an unfamiliar feeling. Often they've returned from summer adventures overexposed to the sun and underdressed for the night. You'd think, with their combined IQs, they could plan ahead better, but it's a way, she thinks, of clinging to what little remains of their youth. In another year—damn!—she'll have to get a full-time job.

From somewhere among the trees, an animal cry reaches them, loud enough to freeze everyone in place. Surprised by its sudden arrival and its otherworldly pitch, Karalee feels a tightness at the base of her throat.

"What the hell was that?" Josh asks.

"The Cropsey Maniac," says Estela. "Boo!"

"Who's the Cropsey Maniac?" asks Gerard.

"Your brother," Chick snaps.

"Never mind," says Josh. "She's referring to an old campfire story. He was an escaped lunatic, I think—in the story. Well, it loses its bite if you have to ask."

"Yeah," Chick says, distracted. "Back here on earth? That sounded like a large bird."

They all cock an ear. If they concentrate, in fact, there are plenty of things to hear all around them—nature sounds from their immediate surroundings as well as those from far away, amplified by the river. The roar of a boat horn drifts toward them. Hard to gauge the distance, but Karalee figures that it has to be far off. She's heard boat horns close up, and they can be deafening.

After standing for another minute and listening, they sense that there's nothing to be done about the noises and they filter back into a line heading for the boat. Soon the footing becomes uneven again from the tangle of roots and ground-hugging vines. Karalee concentrates so hard on not turning an ankle that it surprises her when they pop out onto the riverbank. With the setting sun well behind them, they are still in the shadow of trees, but more light permeates out here, reflecting off the surface of the river. For a moment, however, Chick and Gerard obstruct her view. So she's not sure what's going on when the epithets begin flowing.

"Holy crap!"

"Sonuvabitch!"

"What the—?"

She slips off her sneakers and steps out into cold water halfway up her shins and sees for herself. Their boat is filled with cloudy water. Swamped. The floating coolers and the ruined first aid kit—saturated packages of gauze, soggy Band-Aid boxes, foil-wrapped aspirins turned to paste—and a few articles of clothing bat against one another as if they have a life of their own.

At first she can't process it. None of them can.

"Did it rain?" Josh says idiotically, although that had been Karalee's initial thought, too.

"No, it didn't rain," Chick says with an edge of sarcasm. "Shit." He climbs over the port-side gunwale and sloshes about, peering down. "Hard to see."

"You got a flashlight in the glove compartment?"

"Negative, Gerry. Remember our last adventure when it died near West Point? Meant to replace the batteries. Never did. Maybe the running lights." He flicks a toggle by the dashboard, but nothing happens.

Gerard holds out his Bic and snaps it into flame, lowers it to a few inches above the level of the water. Karalee can see the orange-blue reflection of the flame, but it scarcely penetrates. She pulls out her camera and ignites the flash, but the light won't linger long enough to accomplish anything.

"There must be a hole in the hull," Chick reasons. "I guess we went in harder than I thought when we landed. Hell! We were in such a hurry to disembark. If we'd only noticed sooner!"

He frantically drops to his knees in the water and sloshes around like a madman, feeling for the break, then jumps to his feet, dripping, and kicks at the surface of the water in anger. He issues a string of curse words, pulls at his ponytail, finally rests his fingertips on his temples and runs through a series of deep breaths and exhalations to regain his composure. Then he goes to try the radio, but no indicator light comes on. Rather than acknowledge that fact, he speaks into it anyway. "Mayday! Mayday! This is the *Flagellum*, a Boston Whaler on the East River by North Brother Island. Mayday! Mayday!"

"That radio looks dead," Estela says, unmoved by his show of frustration.

"It is dead," Chick admits. "Must've shorted out."

"So why are you talking into it?"

Chick sighs and carelessly drops the microphone. "Any bright ideas, my fellow geniuses?"

Gerard stares out at the river and Karalee follows his gaze. Darkness is falling fast now. Lights have come on in the Bronx and glow from passing boats. But they can see no activity anywhere close to them. It's already too dark to assess the state of the fire by Hunts Point. In the fading light, clouds of smoke and ordinary clouds have all blended to dull mottled gray.

"My suggestion is toke some dope," Gerard says. "Also, I have a few Quaaludes in my pocket that we all can share."

"Get serious," Josh says.

"I am. What's the point of fretting right now? We can camp in the woods for the night. We'll have a lot better chance of getting someone's attention come daybreak."

"For Christ's sake!" Chick cries.

They hear a heavy motor and spot a tugboat chugging through the gloaming. Estela and Josh leave the water and climb to a small rise, where they begin jumping up and down, crying out. "Here! Over here! Help!"

"Save your breath," Karalee says. From her vantage point, it's obvious that the trees will hide them from anyone on the river, especially in fading light. And there's no way a person on that noisy boat would hear their voices anyway. It goes without saying, but she does anyway: "That tugboat is like half a mile away."

There are stories about this place, whispered among those who ply New York's waters and passed along to Karalee half in jest by her mother. Stories about faces glimpsed in hospital windows. About eerie lights out on the shore. About mysterious voices calling through darkness.

Regardless of their truth, the stories carry their own power. No professional boat captain steers himself within hailing distance of North Brother Island.

Mary

MARY PACES QUIETLY in the upstairs hallway of the pavilion, easily avoiding the debris that litters the floor. She is accustomed to darkness after all these years. The artificial lights dimmed forever long ago, and she never lights a fire in open air or near a window, lest she call attention to her presence and invite more upon herself than the inconvenience caused by mischievous prowlers.

There have been vandals, now and then, for as long as she can remember, adventure seekers yearning to leave a mark at someone else's expense. When they come, she scares them away in the subtlest manner, never revealing herself, only sending a hunk of plaster tumbling dangerously or a bottle sailing with malice off a shelf.

Everyone who presses a toe into the loam of the island senses its possession by the shaded world, but they cannot know precisely how it is haunted. Let them think it is a poltergeist, she always figures, something that merely threatens a blow to the head or a bad tumble down the stairs. As if that were the worst that could befall a person here.

If only that were the worst of it, maybe Mary herself could lay down her head in peace. What she faces and has always battled is far more trying: the ugly truth of undying inequity. Here it is in her ragged clothes, her bare feet. There it is in the cries of those who yearn for justice but will never find it.

In any event, she does not ever show herself to the intruders, yet always manages to scare them off. Usually she goes up to the topmost window and watches them making haste from the island, no doubt regretting that they have not heeded the off-limits warnings. Oh, she knows about the island's status despite not having uttered a word to a living person in decades. She has heard the park rangers talking of it on their rare visits. And the trespassers. But mostly she can tell by the paucity of visitors and how surreptitiously they arrive.

These ones today are different, though. They are the ones that Mathilde foretold. Mary felt it the moment she sat up in bed. And their own words confirmed it.

They think they know her. She knows them better, because they are like all the rest who have tormented her. She heard it in their voices, the big words they used. Too smart for their own good . . . or anyone's.

The Soper girl. So close. That is the one thing she could not believe at first. But on reflection, it makes perfect sense that the Soper girl should come. She has a family interest. A strand connects her to Mary. Compared to her, the others among today's intruders are only a nuisance. But if the Soper girl did not come today, she would have come tomorrow.

Mary walks through the building following their trail. She has developed powers over all these years that she never would have imagined possessing back in the day when she arrived as a frightened teenager to the big hall on another island—Ellis Island. Perhaps in part these powers are associated with her condition, a complement to her imperviousness. And in part perhaps they have been refined by the conditions in which she lives.

Alert now, she feels an inner strength like never before, tracking the path that the Soper girl cut through the pavilion.

Traces of the girl's warmth remain.

Her scent lingers.

Mary follows it from the cafeteria to the kitchen and back out. She follows it into the old laboratory. Night has fallen, but a few rays of light from the rising moon enter through the windows. Just enough light for Mary to see the specimen box there on the counter.

They touched it, the nosy bastards!

She picks it up, wants to heave it out the window in anger. But its contents came from her, and therefore it is a part of her. She will not think now how he took the specimens from her, vile Soper. She who has spent so much time worrying over the past will think only of the future now. Thus she closes her eyes in the darkness, strains to put a face to the Soper girl's voice.

The image will not yet come, but she will know her before long. She is sure of it. There are few ways off this island for the living. Even fewer for the dead.

Karalee

THE MOON RISES early, nearly full. On open ground its beams might glisten off foreheads and noses and glint in her friends' eyes, but the weary autumn leaves of the trees block the moonlight as they blocked the sunlight, creating heavy nighttime shade. As a result, Karalee can see the others only in silhouette. And of course, the moon casts no warmth. Huddled together in darkness by the riverbank, they've all begun to shiver. None of them will freeze to death out in the woods tonight, she supposes, but the breeze has a bite to it, and the discomfort will only worsen.

Chick must be thinking the same thing. "There's no point staying outside with all this shelter around," he says. "If we go back to the pavilion, at least we can find relief from the wind."

"I'm game." Estela hugs herself. She grabbed a T-shirt from the boat, but it's wet, so she won't put it on. "One of those old wards had a few cots and mattresses scattered around. Maybe we can even find the remains of a blanket or two. Kind of gross, but as the saying goes, any poor in a storm."

"That's 'port'—any port in a storm," Josh says without humor. Estela sticks out her tongue at him.

When Karalee considers the sleeping arrangements that Estela describes, an unsettling picture clarifies in her mind. In her recurring nightmares, she senses something soiled beneath her. She can never bring herself to look, but she recognizes it as the source of a revolting odor—she can almost smell it now in her imagination. She rubs the itchy tip of her runny nose with a knuckle. The idea of going back inside the pavilion and attempting to bed down in the filth sends her into a cold sweat.

"I don't know," she says. "It was dirty and creepy in there, and at night it must be creepier."

"What choice do we have?" Josh asks. "There's no tents, and I didn't see a Holiday Inn sign anywhere on this island. Accommodations are extremely limited."

"Aw," Chick says, looking to Karalee. "You're freezing." He puts a warm arm around her and pulls her close. It's only the second time he has touched her since last night, and it does feel better. "You can't stay out here for the next twelve hours."

"Twelve whole hours?"

"Dawn to dusk. Dusk to dawn. Equinox. Tomorrow is the first day of fall."

She shivers more deeply at the thought. "I forgot about that. Okay. But let's make the best of it. There's the ice cream and hot dogs." Comfort food, she's thinking.

"But the cold . . ."

"We'll build a campfire in the plaza in front of the pavilion," Estela suggests.

"Grab what's left of the beers," Gerard adds. "Use it to wash down the Quaaludes."

Chick waves a hand. "We're not doing Quaaludes, dude." A long pause as they all stare at him. "At least, not until we get there. Who's gonna help me with these coolers?"

Gerard and Chick climb back into the boat and dump the melted-ice water from the beer cooler, passing it down to shore along with the one full of food. They grab what else they can, mostly wet T-shirts, and divide the work. Estela carries the extra clothes in a canvas tote she had on board, save the one T-shirt, which she waves around in an effort to dry it.

Gerard hoists the food cooler onto his shoulder.

Karalee shares the burden of the beer cooler with Josh. Being nearly empty, it's light, but the cans crash around inside, shifting the weight back and forth.

They decide to pass by the area of the chopping block, with the idea that they can gather wood there for a fire.

"This is awesome," Chick says, genuinely trying to make the best of it. "We're like survivalists."

"Yeah, but the world hasn't come to an end," Josh says. "It's just out there. Across the river." Passing clouds now partially obstruct the moon, and the lights of Manhattan paint the sky silver.

"So close, yet so far," Estela intones.

A few of them laugh over it. What else is there to do?

They chuff along. In eight minutes they come to the spot in the woods where the clearing with the chopping block ought to be, but they can't find it.

"We went off course in the darkness," Chick admits.

They put the coolers down and fan out in a circle, but when they lose sight of one another among the trees, he calls them all back. "It's not worth it."

"I could swear that thing was here," says Gerard.

"We don't need to build a campfire," Estela says. "It was just a nice idea."

After no more than a few strides, Karalee spots the pavilion looming in front of them. As they emerge into the remains of the plaza, the moon gains the upper hand over parting clouds, casting a wash of warm light on the grand old building. She's already so sick of the woods and the chill that it almost feels like home. She sets down her end of the cooler for a moment and takes a picture of the pavilion's disintegrating façade with the moonlight falling upon it, bracing her elbows against her torso in an effort to hold the camera still for the long exposure, the *click-click* seeming to take forever.

Waste of a shot, probably blurred, she concedes. She changes her settings and turns on the flash and snaps a few quick candids of the Sewer Rat gang. Then they pick up the coolers again and continue walking.

They cross the remains of the plaza and set down their things again by the front entrance for a rest. With moonlight falling through the glass ceiling, the atrium glows ethereally.

"This isn't so bad," Gerard says, stretching out his arm muscles and loosening his back.

The breeze quiets here and so do the noises from the river. Across the plaza, an old lamppost, still straight as rain, catches Karalee's eye. She can imagine the lamp, years ago, casting a pool of soft amber light. She can imagine recuperating patients walking side by side on a sticky summer night, engaged in conversation, perhaps anticipating their release back into the wide world.

A shadow moves in the vicinity of the post, cast by a passing puff of cloud. Or so she thinks at first, but then the shadow appears to become strangely animate.

It's moving. A form of some kind. A human form.

She lifts the camera to her eye and attempts to zoom in, but suddenly can't locate it. Just her eyes playing tricks, it seems. She drops the camera to her hip.

"Let's get inside. I'm cold."

GUIDED BY MOONLIGHT that filters through dirty and broken windows, they plod their way cautiously up the central stairs and along gloomy interior hallways. Eventually, they arrive at the ward Estela remembered with the cots.

Chick, first to the door, comes up short.

"What is it?" Josh asks from behind.

"I don't know. This wasn't like this."

They huddle in the doorway, craning their necks. The moon provides good light inside this room, easy to see what's going on. Four cots stand in a row, parallel to one another, mattresses splayed on top. But that's not all. Pillows lie atop the mattresses at the heads of the beds.

Karalee's stomach flutters.

"Holy shit," Estela says, although it comes out "Holy sheet." No one laughs at the inadvertent pun. In any case, the beds have no sheets, the pillows no pillowcases. It's all institutional stripes.

Chick spins around. "You guys are messing with me, right?" he whines. "When I was walking in the lead down the hall earlier today, one of you or—no—" He holds up a finger. "—two of you, because it's only funny if someone else is in on the gag, right? You snuck back and arranged this like this."

"Why would we?" Gerard says. "We had no idea we were coming back."

"Yeah, like, ever," Josh emphasizes.

Chick takes ahold of Gerard's bulky upper arms and goes nose to nose with him. "I don't know. But you are messing with me, right? It has to be."

"Someone is," Josh says, running his fingers through his hair and adjusting his glasses on his nose with a pinky.

They're still huddled by the doorway. Karalee raises her camera above Estela's right shoulder and zooms in on one of the pillows. Sees something. Zooms into another pillow and sees the same thing. A rectangular-shaped package of some kind, hints of shininess, but hard to make out any distinctions through a lens in filtered moonlight. It's all grainy.

A crashing sound from behind them cracks the silence. They let out a collective scream and dance through the door shoulder to shoulder, maintaining physical contact. The nerve endings tingle in Karalee's torso, spiders fanning out to crawl all over her. She wipes madly at her arms.

"Calm down!" Chick says. "Everyone calm down!"

"Are you serious?" Josh asks. "That's the last thing we should do."

Chick gets in his face now. "And what's the first?"

"We gotta get the hell out of here, that's what."

"No." Chick bites a thumb knuckle and shakes his fist. "Think about it. That's what they want—whoever did this. They set this up to creep us out."

"Who did?" Karalee asks.

"The greenhouse keeper. The person maintaining that garden. There's someone living on this island, and they want us gone."

"Oh, like every plot in *Scooby-Doo*, right? And that noise up the hall?"

"I dunno. Something hitting the floor. The building is falling apart. But we can't leave until daybreak. And it's still safer here inside four walls than it is out there in the woods with an ax on the loose."

"An ax!" Josh cries, throwing up his hands. "You had to bring that up!"

"He's right, though," Estela says. "We're safe here. Four walls. Just two doors, and that one appears to be nonfunctional."

"Yeah, no doorknob and painted shut. Where do you suppose it once led?"

"Damned if I know. And I'm not planning to find out," Chick says. "It looks tight. With luck, it's frozen shut like those garage doors in the boathouse seemed to be. But either way, whoever tends that garden knows. We've been here not half a day. They've had who knows how long to study this place."

"We're five people," Gerard says. "We can keep an eye on two doors." Leading with his chest, he strides across the room, moving through moonlight to shadow and back again. He gingerly lifts the unidentified thing off the first pillow and holds it up to the moonlight, brings it to his nose and gives it a sniff. "Yodels."

"What?" Josh walks up to him. They all push deeper into the room.

"Yodels. 'Frosted Creme Filled Devil's Food Cakes,'" Gerard reads from the package, grinning like a fool. He holds the package aloft again. "Can't see the expiration date in this light." Sniffs some more. "Still smells good."

Chick snatches the package from him. "Don't be an ass, Gerry. You're not eating that. No one is eating that."

"Why not?" Gerard picks up a package from another pillow. "I'm sure they came from the pantry. Whether the person who put them here has bad intentions or not, they're in sealed packages."

"No way. I'm pulling rank here. As your professor," Chick says, grabbing for the second package.

Gerard evades him, holding the Yodels at arm's length and blocking with his other forearm. "Yeah, some professor. Led us out here with no

life jackets in the middle of Hell Gate and didn't think to bring a working goddamn flashlight."

The back of Chick's neck darkens and an eye twitches. He shrugs,
hands over the first package, too. "Suit yourself."

"Chick!" Josh says. "You're not gonna let him."

"He's a big boy."

"He's a big boy," Gerard says, tearing the package open, "and the pantry
is a long damn way off. And the hot dogs are frozen. And he's starving."

They watch him tear the package open and take a bite of the first
Yodel. He swallows it quickly and everyone waits for him to die.

TWO HOURS HAVE passed and Gerard lives, high as the smokestack on
the other side of the island. They all are. High and hungry, the Yodels
all eaten, jokes about full turn-down service fading into the night.

The moon, nearly full, has moved halfway across the sky.

Karalee, sitting on the cot next to Chick, has progressed from giggles
to the slow burn of paranoia. She tries without success not to think about
the condition of the mattress beneath her. Although it has stains so dark
she can see them clearly in monochrome filtered moonlight, she'd like
to figure that it's still ten steps up from sleeping on the floor tonight.
Then again, so would a used casket be. Chick, upon seeing the mattress
up close, made a menstruation joke, but Karalee's sanity relies on convincing herself that they are only water stains.

No one else's mattress looks much better, and their condition doesn't
only skeeve out Karalee; it depresses her. Long ago, she thinks, these items
must have arrived here new and promising, as this place once was—meant
to address a societal need, built with great expectations. A public work
that projected ambition right down to its architectural flourishes. Now
look at it!

They once treated people *as people* here, she thinks. The patients were
outcasts, yes, but not prisoners. Save one.

In her mind's eye, she again sees the famous picture of Mary Mallon, one of a dozen patients twisting around in bed to look at the photographer. Typhoid Mary. That photo could not have been taken in this ward, she recalls, as the Tuberculosis Pavilion was built after Mary's death, the last major building constructed here. And yet it may as well have been taken here or in any of the once-sterile rooms in a dozen buildings now shrouded in filth and decay. This building or that . . . this room or another . . . these tiles . . . that bit of architectural ornamentation—what difference do surface details make to the person who experiences the whole island as a prison?

A spring in the cot beneath her groans, and Karalee recaptures her train of thought, once more contemplates that photograph, shot more than fifty years ago. No doubt all those grown adults in the picture are now dead, she thinks.

Ashes to ashes.

She looks at the dust that coats the floor and windowsills—so thick, it is visible through the gloom.

Gerard rises from his cot and walks to the coolers that they left by the doorway. He reaches to open one. "Man, I forgot there's also ice cream in here."

"Not yet," Karalee says, feeling uncharacteristically proprietary. "It's mine. I'm saving it until we're desperate."

"Suit yourself. I'm close to eating those wieners cold." Gerard smirks at his friends. "No gay jokes. Didn't mean that the way it came out. Aw, hell." He snorts as he opens the other cooler. "Three beers left. Just enough to wash down the Quaaludes. Who's game?"

They all are—even Karalee. When she raises a hand, Chick tucks his chin and opens his eyes wide. "It's a long night," she explains, "and I'm not planning to be the only one who spends it sober."

Estela breaks into song: "Whatever gets you through the ni-ight . . ."

"It's all right!" the Sewer Rats sing off-key. "It's all right!"

Gerard places two pills, smaller around than a dime and maybe six times thicker, in the center of her palm. In the gray light, she can't discern their true color for sure. A pastel of some kind, as benign-looking as aspirins or SweeTarts.

She pops them into her mouth without another moment's hesitation and washes them down with two gulps of warm Bud.

After a while, she feels like lying down but finds Chick in the way. Although the edge has come off both her paranoia and her OCD, she's still not eager to touch the pillow, so she welcomes Chick's chest. He wraps his arms around her, and she feels his breath in her hair. It seems to come from far off, but it tickles her to sleep.

WHEN SHE WAKES up, it is still night. Other than making that observation, she has no idea how long she's been out.

Quiet commotion fills the room, her friends shuffling about, getting ready to go. She's not sure whether she's dreaming. If so, at least it's not her usual nightmare of the cage—that's what it is! A cage, not a jail. Wire, not bars.

"What's going on?" she says, sitting up. "Where are we going?"

"Down," Estela says. "To the pantry for food."

"How long was I asleep?"

"I don't know. Ten minutes?"

Estela's voice doesn't sound right. It's coming to Karalee through a tunnel of distortion, like a Doppler effect but with no one moving fast enough to create such a thing. More like slow motion, in fact.

"Is everyone going?" Karalee asks.

They don't answer—or they answer and she doesn't hear. She becomes aware that Chick has left the cot and she's facing the backs of a bunch of people. Four people, although it seems to take forever to count them. They are all moving away from her toward the doorway.

She jumps from the cot. "Hey, wait up."

Voices around her. Laughing. Goofy. Childlike voices drifting toward her from far away. Her group occupies the hallway, their voices echoing. She feels them shifting places all around her and thinks of three-dimensional diagrams of atoms—electrons rotating around a nucleus. Yet she doesn't really feel like the center of things. More like someone carried along on a cloud.

At the same time, she knows she really is carrying herself along. She stares down at her feet, which are moving. Left right left right. The tips of her canvas sneakers have become stained. Although she can barely see six inches in front of her, somehow she can see this. They have disgusting tea-colored stains, tattooed there in uneven splotches, and the rubber toes are accumulating globs of dust.

Her feet have their own volition. She watches them rise and fall. Left right left right. Like the pistons on a machine at an amusement park. Maybe that's where she is. Rye Playland. Excited voices all around her, too. But, no, she is in the Tuberculosis Pavilion. She remembers that. She took a picture not long ago.

Her camera! Suddenly she becomes aware that she left it behind. An unbearable thought. She has to go back.

She lifts her numb hand to her left ear, where the scar tingles. Runs her fingers back and forth over it. Her father threw the camera at her and it shattered. The camera is no more. But then she recalls the counter at the camera store, where she bought the new one on layaway. Still staring at her feet, she tells her friends that they have to double back for the camera, but they ignore her or they don't hear. Maybe her lips are moving but nothing is coming out. She wants to lift her gaze from her sneakers but it's so hard, like moving a mountain. She wants to scream, but as she does so, it's like her experience during the nightmares, the sound dying in her lungs, never making it to her vocal cords. Finally, the words are about to emerge when her friends spread out away from her. She didn't notice descending stairs but they must have gone down, because they're on a different floor now. The room is much larger than the hallways but only marginally better lit.

Just as she looks up, everyone starts closing ranks again. They are shoulder to shoulder, brushing up against one another. Karalee's skin crawls, but she can't push them away. She senses their great trepidation, strains to focus her attention across the big dark room.

From a corner of the massive kitchen, a form comes into view in the murk. It moves slowly but deliberately in their direction, following an invisible diagonal.

"Is it a spirit?" Estela whispers, dead serious, eyes wide.

Karalee senses shallow breathing around her, but she thinks instead of the well-tended greenhouse garden. She finds her voice. "It's that caretaker Chick was talking about."

They take not a step in the form's direction, peer through semi-darkness to discern more details.

"He's alone," says Gerard.

"Park ranger?" Chick speculates.

"At this hour?" Josh wonders, an edge to his voice.

"It's not that late," Gerard says. "It's just dark."

In truth, Karalee suspects that Gerard has no more idea what time it is than she does. He retrieved the watch, but she hasn't seen him look at it. Like all of them, he's fixated on the person who approaches.

As the figure nears, walking slowly, Karalee starts to see details, and a space opens up inside her. The form has a masculine walk but wears flowing garments that suggest some sort of skirt. "It's a woman," she says, noting how that observation relaxes everyone.

"Hello," Chick calls when the woman is ten paces away.

A gust of wind comes through an open window, catching the woman's garments. Karalee, feeling a chill, slips her hands into her pockets and hunches her shoulders.

In a moment, the woman is fully upon them, stopping just beyond arm's reach. She is dressed in rags but has a proud bearing, broad shoulders drawn back, an oval face with high cheekbones. She smells sour, like rancid oil, and her dark hair is a wild nest. She has a strong chin. In the darkness, Karalee discerns little more than that.

"What brings you here?" the woman asks without greeting.

"Uh." Chick fumbles. "Boat trouble."

Karalee can see his drug-addled mind working, grinding as slowly as her own. The woman is no park ranger for sure. And if she's the island's caretaker, her superiors haven't checked on her in a very long time.

Meanwhile, judging from the angle of her head—Karalee can't see her eyes in the dark—she appears to be studying them. "No one ever comes here but vandals."

"We mean no harm," Chick says, as if he's talking to an alien creature on a planet they've just discovered. "How long have you been here? Do you go with the island?"

"Ay." The woman has gravel in her voice and an accent of some kind. "In a manner of speaking. Boat trouble, you say?"

"Well, honestly, not boat trouble at first," Estela says. "We came into this part of the river because there was a big fire somewhere in the Bronx. Some police and Coast Guard boats passed us, hurrying that way. We followed them and the smoke—to see what was going on."

The woman nods. Out of focus—all motion nothing but streaks of gray in Karalee's sight. "I might have seen something of that sort out across the river," the woman concedes.

"We saw the island and thought, why not check it out? We're not vandals." Estela hesitates. "I hope we haven't disturbed you."

The woman fails to answer.

"Do you live here?" Estela pursues.

"Ay. I do." A terrible odor wafts over. Even at some distance and filtered through Karalee's own foggy detachment, the woman's breath nearly overpowers her. She feels compelled to place it, however: the aroma of blue cheese . . . of barf . . . of garlic . . . of something rancid. She chokes back a gag.

"Where's your house?" Estela asks.

"Abouts," the woman says, frowning. "You from the census or are you just nosy?"

It's an Irish accent, Karalee thinks dully. A round Irish accent with American edges cut into it.

"We don't work for the government," Josh says. "We're academics, curious people. We study things. Are you homeless?"

The woman takes a long time to answer, poring over their faces in the dark. Her gaze seems to linger on Karalee. Then she looks out past them all toward the trees through the greasy window. "Not homeless, no. Everything you see is my home."

"Are you all alone here, then?" Estela asks.

With her silence, the woman resists their curiosity. Karalee feels an absence, a vacuum, as if the woman just left the room and no air arrived to fill the space she vacated. But she is still here, and her posture gives up her secret, answers in the affirmative.

Yes, it says. *Yes. Even in your presence, I am very much alone.*

SHE IS A hermit, Karalee surmises. The hermit of North Brother Island. In this big city, it makes perfect sense that the island would tempt someone seeking solitude without having to travel too far. Hermits may check out of society, but they often live within spitting distance of its conveniences. They glean off of it for survival.

That is the logical thread that Karalee follows, anyway. Every thought spans a great distance in her head, as if her brain has two different parts with a void in between. She opens her mouth to speak, aware from the first syllable that her speech slurs, but presses on.

"How did—how did you get here?" she asks the woman.

"By boat, same as everyone else. 'Tis the only way."

"Do you mind if we stay the night?" asks Estela.

"Just until we get our boat fixed tomorrow morning," Josh adds.

The woman's mind appears to be churning. No doubt, thinks Karalee, she is unaccustomed to extensive human contact. Otherwise, she'd live elsewhere. Anywhere but here. In addition, she is likely mentally ill, like so many homeless. Or on drugs—like Karalee and the rest of them. At the thought of that, she almost giggles, covers her mouth with her fingertips.

Her own fingers smell musty.

"It's a free country," the woman replies to Estela. "Supposed to be." Her gaze rakes over them some more, calculating. "Academics, you say?"

"From Havermeyer University. The School of Public Health?"

Karalee nudges Estela, trying to communicate that a homeless woman can't be expected to know what she's talking about.

As if to confirm that assumption, the woman says absently, "Public health." She mulls for a long moment. "Where's that?"

"Up Poughkeepsie way," Chick says. "These guys are graduate students and I'm one of their professors."

"We should introduce ourselves," Estela says. They tell her their names. No handshakes. Karalee again suppresses a gag at the smell of the woman, forces it out of her mind. The woman doesn't share her name, and no one presses. Karalee feels like a drunk who has stumbled into the wrong hotel room only to watch the occupants sit up startled in bed. She may not be far from the truth on that.

Gravid silence follows, and the woman herself breaks it. "You can't spend the night on an empty stomach. I'll feed you."

An awkward pause. Shuffling of feet. The appearance of the Yodels on the cot pillows floats up to Karalee. The woman might have a kind heart beneath her gruffness, an element of humanity underneath the rags and the odor. Layers. She looks down to see that the woman's feet are bare and her stout toes are black with dirt.

She turns her attention from the toes to her own soiled sneakers. In between, the cloudy floor begins to spin, an effect of the Quaaludes. She grabs Chick's arm for balance, hears his voice arrive thick through the air.

"It was nice of you to provide the beds, ma'am," he says. "But no need to trouble about dinner. We'll just bed down, quiet as mice. And be on our way in the morning." There's a tremble in his voice—Karalee picks up that much through the miasma that seems to surround her. He must be freaking out just as the drugs thoroughly take over.

"Quiet as a mouse?" The woman frowns, preparing to rebuke him. "A mouse is noisy enough if you know how to listen," she says. "You'll be starving by morning and I have plenty. I'll feed you, I will. I insist. There's a whole meal already made, fresh today."

"Fresh?" Josh half whispers.

At once Karalee can smell it, rich and meaty, riding a crest of steam across the kitchen. Well, look at that: A pot simmers on the stove. It dawns on her that Chick was right all along: The stove works. Her stomach puckers as her senses process the cooking aroma. She rubs her tired eyes, and when she opens them again, the woman is staring at her.

"This dish will put some heat in you," she says. "And we'll make a nice fire, too. Warm you right up. So warm, could be, that you'll hardly be able to stand it."

Mary

It is the Soper girl, all right. She can tell that much, feels the tingle at the back of her neck, akin to the feeling she gets when a rat stumbles into one of her traps in the woods. Of all the times she has had that feeling, she has never once found an empty trap.

These students—if that is what they are—look strange to her, however. Too accepting. Glassy-eyed. Distant. Could they be different kinds of ghosts from the ones to whom she has grown accustomed? Ghosts arrayed in modern clothing? Or could they be figments of her imagination?

But that boat behind the seawall was solid enough when she took her ax to it, and that thing surely did not steer itself to her shore. So they must be real people. And they carry an air that would offend her under any circumstances. Worse now that she knows for sure what they are about, curiosity seekers at her everlasting expense.

And the Soper girl. The Soper girl! *The Soper girl!* She trembles to visualize the terrible thread that began in the loins of George A. Soper and grew like a tapeworm through the generations.

Mary peers over her shoulder at the visitors as she stirs the rabbit stew on the kitchen stove. When earlier she brought the pot down from its hiding place, she saw that the students in their prying left a burner knob open. She smiles now thinking of it. Young fools did that, not ghosts.

They could not know about the shutoff valve to the gas line she always uses, around to the side of the equipment and behind.

The students stare at her from across the kitchen. She feels their dewy eyes on her back. They drool at the scent of her lovely stew. With her heightened senses, she can almost hear the saliva drip. She will not turn around just now, directs her mind instead to memory of her forced visit to the hospital on Sixteenth Street. They held her down, they did, the orderlies under Dr. Baker's direction, in order to draw blood.

But she was strong.

When she saw the needle come out, she writhed so that they chose to strap her to a hard chair with leather restraints, her blouse torn in the process, her left arm eventually laid bare and vulnerable, wrist facing up.

"Open your hand, Mary," Dr. Baker instructed. "Relax your arm."

Instead she closed her muscular hand into a fist, held it fast in a ball. Her last measure of resistance. An orderly worked to pry her fingers apart but could not. She looked him in the eye, gritted her teeth.

Two of them tried together, one finger at a time. She had her short nails digging into the heel of her own hand so tight that red fluid began to seep forth.

There is your blood. On my own terms.

They attempted with the needle to penetrate her forearm regardless. So enraged was she that she barely felt it then. The nurse broke the skin, but the needle bent, caught in rigid muscle. The nurse withdrew the device and held it up, showing Dr. Baker, who pursed her lips and shook her head.

On her instructions, the orderlies persisted. Two of them. Strong men, pulling on Mary's sturdy fingers.

Mary held fast, her fists clenched as tightly as her teeth.

Then the smaller of the two orderlies, a freckled redhead named O'Connor whose parents probably came directly from the old sod, got a devilish look in his arctic-blue eyes. With Dr. Baker and the nurse looking away, debating what to do, he reached down between Mary's legs and pinched her in a spot that none but Briehof had ever touched.

She gasped. It took all her strength not to cry out, not to give him the satisfaction of that victory. Her legs snapped closed but her hands unclenched.

Immediately the orderlies flattened her left palm open. "Hurry!" one urged the nurse, who produced a fresh needle, holding it point up as she approached.

That needle! Mary had never visited a doctor in her life. Never yielded control of herself to the whims of others. The pinch to her privates was insult enough. When that needle entered her, it punctured her very soul.

Finally, they had one of their three samples. One only. Later, alone in the locked hospital room, the specimen jars sat empty for a second day. She continued to insist on flushing the toilet against their wishes. Soper came in with a janitor, his eyebrows raised, his gaze determined. She looked at him with hatred, sat on the bed with her arms folded across her chest, attempting to anticipate his next move.

The janitor went into the bathroom and emerged a minute later. Soper, without a word, just a cold stare over his shoulder, followed him out. Mary heard the door to the hall lock but tested it anyway. She examined the bathroom. How stupid did they think she was? The janitor had turned off the water to the toilet but had not removed the shutoff-valve knob. When she needed to go again, she opened the line with a few turns of the knob and resumed flushing.

But she lay abed in dark despair. She knew Soper and his cohorts would prevail eventually. They had all the power, had demonstrated that much when they extracted her blood.

And the memory of that feeling—or was it more than a memory; had it never gone away, even for a second?—salted the open wound of her indictment against George A. Soper. For as she now looks over that Soper girl and her friends, all she can think is how normal they appear. As had the girl's hard-hearted great-grandfather long ago. For when Mary lay in that hideously pristine hospital bed, confined in a room so sterile it almost served, in and of itself, as an act of aggression against her, she thought how Soper did casual violence to her in the morning and went home to his fine family in the afternoon. How he passed through the streets in his three-piece suit with his pocket watch and his spectacles, carrying his smugness like a badge while she lamented the loss of what little she had: her independence, her freedom, control over her own person.

In her view today, the legacy of Soper's careless power now lives on in these students who intrude upon her island. She sees, even glassy-eyed, that they are so normal and Mary is so different. Yet—she smiles—their normalcy makes them most vulnerable to the predations she considers. Their stupor further clears the way for advancement of her plans. Even on their best day, they are likely so blinded by their own privilege that they cannot fathom what she is capable of doing when provoked. And of course, she has long been provoked.

Furthermore, they have now agreed to dinner. However reluctantly, they have begun to trust.

They continue to stare at her back. She spins round on them abruptly. Did they jump? "A watched pot never boils. Do be a pet and proceed to the cafeteria. There." She points to the door with a bent index finger. "Have a seat and I'll be with you."

As they obey, she turns back to stir the pot, thinking she must make a good show of hosting them. So many plates broken over the years that there are only a few intact in the pantry, and the hospital administrators left scarcely any utensils behind when they packed up. Yet she saw more than a few utensils somewhere. . . .

She ponders. It takes her a minute to remember. What she needs lies in a basement room, long forgotten by everyone. Although Mary herself gathered some of the items that reside in that room, she hates to go there. It is an eddy churning with lost souls who have attached themselves to the things that rescue crews picked from the shore long ago—those rescue crews that managed to beat back the scavengers.

As thoughts of the basement room cross Mary's mind, Mathilde surfaces. Mary spots her out the corner of her eye but refuses to acknowledge her. She makes herself busy stirring and stirring the pot.

"Mary."

"Go away. Not now."

"If not now, when?"

There is something different about the apparition today. Mary, unable to resist curiosity, turns fully to her right and sees in an instant, brings a hand to her own mouth and bites hard enough on a finger to taste salty blood. Mathilde's children accompany her. The girl, Friede, nine years old, has a ring of soot around her mouth and nostrils, her eyebrows seared off, her legs stripped of skin. The boy, Adolf, four years old, wears a life preserver, broken in two places and barely clinging to his narrow shoulders. None of the children she infected ever looked so bad. His cheeks are pale blue and his lips have a purple pallor. The eyes stare unblinking.

Mary whispers. "Leave me be, Mathilde."

"But you have it all and we have nothing."

"You don't know what you're talking about. They took everything. I stand empty."

"You live," Mathilde snaps. "The flame burns. What good is a flame that does not singe? Look. Look at them—my precious children."

Mary averts her eyes. "I can't bear it."

"More's the pity. Neither could they." Mathilde snarls. "Use it, Mary. Use what they left you."

Mary stirs and stirs her pot, feeling the weight of Mathilde's stare.

"All this time," the woman says, clutching her children. "Do you know what I am?"

Mary stops stirring, her dripping spoon poised on the lip of the pot. "What? The devil?"

"Hah! You should be so lucky." Mathilde's speech grows slow, a frog in her throat. "I am the shade of lost moments."

"Oh." Upon hearing this, an emptiness, all-consuming, sucks Mary dry. She begins to swoon but catches herself. Her spoon drops to the floor and she picks it up and fixes her eyes on the middle distance.

"We cry for something important. When we're not choking on smoke, we're crying for justice at the tops of our lungs. Yet we remain ever unheard."

"I hear you," Mary says. "All the time."

"What good is to hear if that which is heard goes unanswered? You yourself once cried for justice."

"Once? I cry for it every day."

"And here, before you, lies your chance to put mustard to those cries! They dared to come. Do you dare to do what you must do?"

Mary touches the spoon to her lips, a habitual motion to taste the stew, but she tastes nothing.

"Think, Mary. You won't get this chance again."

"I—I can't." Mary's tears dribble into the pot as she shakes her head. "I am outnumbered, always outnumbered."

"Not today. There are a thousand of us here for you, our strength magnified by circumstance. For once, you are not alone—not as Soper left you."

A groan issues from deep within Mary's chest.

Her lip curls just thinking of the Soper girl's trespass. The Soper girl—just there in the next room. One of that clan so close after all these years.

"Soon," says Mathilde, "she will sit down to dinner. Wasn't that always your strong suit?"

Karalee

THEY TURN FIVE intact cafeteria chairs upright and take seats at the only functional table, resting forward on their elbows. Through heavy eyelids, Karalee observes that the table is not exactly clean but is at least free of dust. She wishes to say the same for herself, but feels creeping indifference. Over the course of less than eight hours on the island, residue from the ruined buildings has laid a coating upon everyone's skin and hair. She drags her tongue across her front teeth to remove a film of grit, and shudders.

"I feel grungy," she admits to Estela.

"Do not expect a shower today," Estela slurs back, her Spanish accent now grown especially heavy. "I try hard to think of this experience as camping out."

Karalee scans the destroyed cafeteria with its missing tiles and cracked plaster and piles of discarded equipment. "More like squatting," she says. "But we have a roof at least."

"There's the *espirit*."

Estela has donned the T-shirt she dragged through the woods, having waved it in the air when she remembered to. Still not completely dry, it is less damp than the others as a result of her efforts. A spare that Josh brought along, it says: JOIN THE ARMY, TRAVEL TO EXOTIC PLACES, MEET

INTERESTING PEOPLE, AND KILL THEM. Estela tugs up the front of the collar and sniffs it, scrunches up her nose.

"Bad?" Karalee asks.

Sheepish grin. "A lot better than some things around here."

"You noticed that, huh?" Karalee whispers. "And we're eating with her."

"I think the ludes suppress the gag reflex."

"Funny."

"I mean it."

The moon has shifted along its arc, casting less light through the cafeteria windows. Karalee can't bear the intense effort required to look into anyone's face. She lets her eyes lose focus, her jaw go slack.

Chick leans in. "You hear that?"

There's a voice filtering through the kitchen door. "It's just the homeless woman," Gerard says.

"Talking to who?" Josh asks.

Karalee strains to listen. She hears only one voice. The woman must be conversing with herself.

The others have drawn the same conclusion. Their speculation retreats back into silence.

"She's nuts," Chick says after a while. "Batty as a bedbug."

"Don't say bedbug!" Josh says. "We still have to sleep tonight."

"Of course she's insane," Estela says. "Who else lives like this but a crazy person?"

"She may be crazy," Gerard says, "but smell that dinner. Even crazy people can have skills. Think Vincent van Gogh. I'm betting the woman in that kitchen can cook."

Gerard puts a can of Budweiser on the table. "Last one." He holds out a fist and opens it to reveal more pills. "And last ones."

They each take their share without further consideration.

Karalee has begun to see colors without clarity in the darkness, some even resembling human forms. Her imagination must be in hyperdrive.

The woman strides in. "There will be rabbit stew if it suits you."

"Rabbit stew? Where do you get your meat?" Josh asks.

She lifts an eyebrow. Can Karalee see that in the dark? She thinks she does, even as she thinks not.

"From the forest. Where else?" Once again, the woman appears to study them. Her look, Karalee suspects, is one of mistrust. "We'll need to scare up some utensils and such. If you'll follow me, a couple of you."

They come to their senses long enough to exchange glances, deciding without a word that they all should go, leave no Sewer Rat behind.

The woman leads them through a door and to the top of a stairwell. "It's the basement," Chick says. "How will we see?"

"I'm used to it," the woman admits. "One grows accustomed. . . ." But when she sees them hesitate further, she concedes. "I do keep some candles for emergencies." She produces a stocky yellowish one from a pocket of her skirt. Finds a box of wooden matches. Lights the wick. "Shall we?"

"You first," Josh mutters.

The woman presses the lit candle upon him. "You take this, then. You all need it more than I."

Without further pause, she disappears into the gloom. When she's almost completely out of their sight, she does stop and peers over her broad shoulder. "If you want to eat in any civilized fashion, you'll have to come. I'm the cook, not the maid."

"I like her spunk," Chick whispers drunkenly. They all choke back a laugh, and he takes the candle from Josh and follows first, with the others close behind.

The basement, from what little Karalee can see in the deep shadows and through her own fog, is a mass of cast-iron pipes and steel beams. It smells of mustiness, and mold grows on the walls, but the space is relatively uncluttered. The woman leads them around several sets of pillars, Karalee thinking of their explorations earlier this afternoon and how much ground they covered. This woman must have every inch mapped in her head.

Still leading them, she comes up short at a storage room deep in the bowels. Chick holds up the candle. Organized chaos lies within, heavily battered objects stacked and sorted on warped wooden shelves. "It looks like a junk shop," Gerard whispers.

The woman mumbles to herself. "Aha. There. I knew I remembered." She points. "See the boxes of plates and forks?"

When Gerard and Josh step forward to gather what the woman needs,

Karalee feels her ears pop, as if the air pressure has dramatically shifted. The woman looks at her, cocking her head, working her jaw side to side with her mouth open. She must feel it, too. But what changed exactly? Nothing Karalee can pinpoint.

Her ears begin to ring. She perceives the objects in the shadows as if through a veil of thin gauze. There are life preservers, coffee urns, ladders, instrument dials, brass musical instruments, metal serving platters—all even grayer than they ought to appear in the poor light. There is a wrought-iron music stand, misshapen, Dalí-like, as if frozen in mid-melt. A bent tin sign that says GENTLEM—the last two letters obscured by soot.

She's about to ask where all of it comes from when the woman turns on her bare heels and walks out. Gerard and Josh carry plates and eating utensils in two open wooden boxes. The others follow empty-handed. Karalee stands alone for a moment, her ears still ringing but in psyche-delic waves of sound that she attributes to the drugs, yet almost as if there were something hidden behind the noise that she should be able to decipher. It sounds like the murmuring clamor of voices, like what they heard from the woman in the kitchen, but a hundred times over.

The candle left the room. Karalee blinks in complete darkness. She sees people standing there, dressed as for a turn-of-the-century Sunday outing, full color, in contrast to the sooted grays and blacks of the items on the shelves. But she can't make out their features or describe their clothing to herself in detail, only has a vague sense of it. They are shapes without form, colors without lines of demarcation. They dance before her in the clamor. Or do they not dance, but writhe? Her breath clutches and a feeling of panic runs through her that nearly collapses her knees and threatens to knock her onto her back. Just then, she feels a tug on her arm from behind . . . someone attempting to drag her.

"What the hell are you doing, Kiki?" It's Chick. "We almost left you."

THE SAVORY AROMA of rabbit stew fills every inch of the large kitchen, and Karalee's stomach tightens with anticipation. The meal that the woman's putting together looks hearty. In addition to the stew, she has managed to bake a loaf of bread, presumably from the flour in the big pantry. Karalee wonders how long this woman could feed herself from the bounty that others left behind.

Working as a team, they create place settings at the table, the candle burning in the center. It casts a modest circle of light in the vast cafeteria, scarcely extending past the backs of their chairs. They sit down, whispering stoned and semi-coherent among themselves, and wait for the cook to produce.

"So," Chick says, "how are we gonna get out of here tomorrow? Any ideas? You think the woman can help us?"

"You kidding?" Josh adjusts himself in his chair. "A homeless woman is going to help us get off this island? If she knew how to get off, would she be here?"

Karalee fights to focus her mind, wondering how the woman arrived in the first place. Shipwrecked? A former worker in the rehab facility who never left? At any rate, she made mention of having seen other people pass through here. She might have opted to depart with them. "Maybe she chooses to stay," Karalee theorizes, half to herself.

"Fine," Gerard argues. "But if she chooses to stay, she can't be putting much thought into how to get off. Which means she's unlikely to have an idea that can help us, which puts us on our own again."

Chick leans back in his rickety chair, eyes half-closed. "Can we pause for a second to consider how surreal this all is? We're about to be served a candlelight dinner by a hermit woman who lives in an abandoned hospital."

"Yeah," says Josh. "The way our luck's going, she probably learned to cook in the hospital cafeteria."

They follow that thought where it's bound to go.

"Stop and slop?"

"Mystery meat?"

"C-section rations?"

"Shit on a shingle?"

Chick shakes his head slowly, rubs his jaw. "You think there really will be rabbits in this stew? Or is that just her imagination?"

"She keeps a helluva garden," Gerard says, "must know something. And, man, the smell of that food!"

"Anything smells good next to her," whispers Estela.

Chick leans forward with a finger over his lips. "Shh! Don't jinx it. We play our cards right, we'll have a story to tell."

"If we ever get home to tell it," Josh says.

"Stop being a killjoy," blurts Karalee, still shivering from her encounter in the basement. As much to convince herself as anyone else, she quickly adds: "We'll send up a signal in the morning and everything will be fine. We're surrounded by civilization here."

"So's Alcatraz," Josh mutters.

The woman bumps through the swinging door with her pot in two bare hands. She places it on the table with a look of satisfaction and immediately begins to spoon stew onto everyone's plate.

Gerard, following his success with the Yodels, doesn't hesitate to take a bite. "Hey, this is good. Excellent, in fact. Thank you very much!" He sops up some gravy with a piece of bread.

"The pleasure is mine," the woman says without smiling. "It's not every day I have visitors."

"How long have you been here?" Estela asks.

The woman sighs. "Long as I can remember, it sometimes seems."

"Well, you want to be here, right? Otherwise, we can help you get off the island."

"Don't be silly." She presses her hands into her thighs as if to stand, but instead takes up her fork and begins to eat.

With the heat of the stew combining with the drugs, Karalee feels as if her head balances on a string. As it wobbles, her gaze desperately seeks a point of concentration. It settles on the woman's fork, which appears to be different from all the others. She lifts her own above the plate and examines it more closely, holds the handle to the candlelight and sees a large *S* engraved near the top. Next to her, it looks as if Chick's fork has the same *S*. She assumes all of those from the trove downstairs have it.

"If I may." Gerard attempts to scoop more stew from the pot. There isn't much left.

The woman works her tongue on the roof of her mouth. "I didn't expect anyone," she says, "and two wild rabbits look pretty scrawny next to your young appetites."

Karalee spots a glint in her eye, maybe a reflection of the candle flame, maybe an illusion—the drugs firing off in her own brain.

"No sweat," Gerard says. "We're grateful for your hospitality." Except that his tongue gets tangled on the last word and he almost bites it off. He looks into his plate, puzzled.

"I can make it up to you with dessert," the woman says. "There's cans and cans of provisions."

Karalee knows it's true, having participated in the raiding of the pantry. At the mention of dessert, she thinks also of the ice cream she's brought. It might still be cold, as no one ever popped the top on the cooler. She mentions it, and the woman nods slowly in acceptance.

Gerard and Chick embrace the idea of finally getting at that ice cream. They light a second candle and run upstairs to fetch the cooler. When they return, Karalee throws open the lid. The first thing she sees is the big barbecue fork resting atop several packages of Hebrew National hot dogs. She flushes with shame. They might have contributed these to dinner if she hadn't been such a hoarder. She mutters something about a cookout as she grabs the fork and packages and sets them aside.

Whether anyone notices, she can't say. Her head swims as she straightens up, and she has to place a hand on the table to keep herself from falling. When she recovers, she sees that the ice cream, which was tightly packed and surrounded by ice, appears mostly still frozen. The woman hunches over it with her hand resting atop one of the containers, a look of astonishment across her face. She holds that pose for so long that Karalee wonders sleepily whether she's having a stroke. "Are you okay?" she asks.

The woman recovers herself. "Ice cream. I can scarcely believe it. There's nothing at all frozen to eat around here, except what I put out on the coldest winter nights—and who wants ice then?" She looks off and cocks her head, as if listening for a train whistle from far away.

"So much there . . . we can each take a container," Gerard says, reaching down.

"Oh, no!" The woman swats his hand away. "We'll do something special with this. We will! Leave it to the cook."

Mary

SHE HAS SENT the students to the boiler house, where she lights her fires, with instructions on how to proceed. They stumbled out with a box of wooden matches—the City workers left behind endless quantities of matches in the pantry—and she hopes they have enough wits about them to find the place and get the fire lit. They talked a lot of nonsense over dinner, almost like they were drunk. Maybe the island is affecting them. Maybe the Soper girl has brought an affliction upon herself and everyone about her.

But never mind any of it; Mary knows she won't lose them.

The ice cream containers lie spread out before her like a revelation. Häagen-Dazs, they say, whatever that means. She strains her memory but concludes that she never heard of it. Yet she loves it at first sight, caresses the containers, opens one, runs a dirty finger through it and licks off every drop of ice cream, finding the taste silky sweet and flowery with vanilla. Her eyes fall closed in ecstasy.

Oh, what luck that it is still cold, that she can do it right!

In a rush she goes to the pantry, casting aside everything in her search for the canned peaches. Every time she laid eyes on them until now, the pictures on the labels of these cans reminded her of what she had lost. So she hid them away, would not touch their contents. Now, oh, but it is too delicious!

The last time she made peach melba was for a group. That was 1915. How many years ago, she does not know, but a lot. She was cooking for the staff at the maternity hospital on Twenty-third Street. There were glass bowls with polka dots that called to her, almost insisted upon being filled with peeled fresh peaches, vanilla ice cream, and raspberry sauce. Her specialty. She had always been great at making it. Everyone who tasted her peach melba ate it up, smacked their lips, cried out for more.

That peach melba proved her undoing, though. Soper sniffed it out, concluded that was the primary source of infection because it went unheated, no killing of the germs.

Nevertheless she had peach melba on the menu every Friday at the staff cafeteria in the maternity hospital. A nice bit of sweetness and silk to follow the fish course. The doctors and nurses and other staff scarfed it down as thoroughly as the families she once served, the Warrens and the Robinsons and all the others.

"You make the best desserts, Miss Brown." They knew her as Mariah Brown; she could not very well use her own name after Soper tainted it. "You'll have to give my wife this peach melba recipe one day."

"Oh!" She laughed. "I couldn't possibly reveal my secret, Doctor. Just know you'll always have something extra to carry you into the weekend."

Something extra indeed. That man died, he did. A delightfully horrible death, nosebleeds and terrible rashes and intestinal pain like he had glass inside him and all the rest. She never did like doctors.

Three days later, Soper and his henchmen led her away in handcuffs, which they did not remove until she stepped off the ferry on North Brother, striding big down the pier, holding her head high. As the ferry rocked on the way over, Mary had resisted despair with every fiber of her being. Come what may, she would not let them crush her spirit—but oh, was that proposition tested over the years.

Here, now, as if reading her mind, the apparitions appear. Mathilde stands there with her children again, each of them looking as pitifully deformed as before. Mary pauses her preparations, closes the cooler lid.

"Leave me to it, Mathilde. I know for sure now what I have to do."

She thinks of the tin box in the laboratory. M. MALLON, it once said on the now-faded tag. A year's worth of samples there, bottled up much time ago and festering ever since.

Karalee

THEY ARE BACK in the boiler house, among the machines with their totem faces.

Chick crunches through pebbles of broken glass to a door that in Karalee's mind represents the mouth. The iron hinges creak when he opens it, vibrations down her spine, everyone giving in to a little squirm. He reaches inside and pinches the fine ash, rubbing it between his fingers. "Thoroughly consumed by the fire. This thing must still be pretty efficient."

"It was meant for a lot more than a small pile of wood," Josh says. "Do you suppose the woman gets any heat into the other buildings with it now?"

Chick shakes his head. Holding the candle aloft, he traces a gargantuan bit of ductwork over to an old sheet-metal box taller than a man. "Big fans pushed the heat through the venting tunnels, and they require electricity."

"So why light the fire here?" Estela wonders. "Why not closer to wherever she stays?"

Chick walks back to the big boiler and holds the candle as high as he can reach, beside where a pipe with a large circumference feeds into the brick chimney block. "That smokestack we saw—what would you say? Twenty stories high?"

"More or less," Gerard agrees.

"A small fire like she's burning, it will dissipate the smoke in that vast thing. Nothing visible makes it out the top."

"But will it draw?"

"She doesn't care. Look at this place. There's plenty of room if the smoke backs up. More important, the fact that she comes to this boiler house for warmth tells us something."

"Yeah? What's that?"

"It tells us she doesn't want to be found."

"Well," Karalee says, "we guessed that already. We promised to light a fire. Do you studs want to get the wood or should I go myself?"

"I never called myself a stud," Josh says. "Not once. Gerard—he's your stud. But I'll help."

Karalee and Estela smirk as the men find their way to a closet behind the ductwork. They bang around for a while, and each returns with several split logs. "Well hidden," Gerard says.

"See previous comment," says Chick.

They drop the logs to the floor with a clatter.

"Let me do it," Estela pleads. "I love making fires."

Using her good hand, she lifts each log one at a time and places it into the furnace that once heated the boiler. When she's constructed her pile, she takes the matchbox from Karalee and tucks it under her bad arm. She has to strike several matches before getting the pile alight, but once she does so, the wood burns well and she smiles.

Estela's pretty face glowing orange in the reflection of the fire—that's a great pose. Karalee reprimands herself for leaving the camera back in the ward. So unlike her. She usually carries that thing everywhere, and especially when the potential for novelty presents itself. But she was wasted when they left—still feels loopy.

They gather around the growing flame, holding their hands out and basking. Karalee didn't realize how cold she felt. Her fingertips tingle. Then she recalls carrying those half-frozen hot dogs all the way over.

"Still hungry?" She holds up the package.

"You bet," Gerard says.

There wasn't enough of the woman's stew to fully satisfy any of them. She uses her barbecue fork to cook the hot dogs two at a time over the furnace fire. By the time the last one is ready, she's so hungry that she doesn't mind plucking it off the fork and eating it with her dirty fingers, wiping the grease on her T-shirt.

When they have satisfied themselves, they sit back on the floor in a semicircle. For a moment, Karalee finds herself wondering reflexively about the dirt she's about to touch—and that's about to touch her. But on the way down, a dizzy spell captures her, and she collapses into the sticky dust. It's unavoidable and she's feeling so mellow all of a sudden. She would flat-out lie down in it if she were alone.

"Where do you suppose this woman is?" Gerard asks.

"She forgot about us." Estela pouts. "And we made such a nice fire for her."

"We built that fire for ourselves," Gerard says. "The dogs hit the spot, but I had my heart set on that ice cream. What do you suppose she's making with it? Chocolate sundaes?"

Karalee closes her eyes. "Did you guys catch the look on her face when she saw that ice cream? She was, like, in seventh heaven."

"So she'll gorge herself on it."

"Don't be silly. It's too much for one person."

"She's loony," Gerard persists. "She'll take a bath in it."

"Does she strike you as the kind of person who bathes?" Karalee immediately feels unkind for saying that.

"I don't know what to make of her," Josh admits. "But I'm glad we found her. I'm less creeped out having another person around who isn't us. It proves that we're still in the world, and it's helping us pass the night."

"Bullshit," Chick says. "It's the drugs that are helping us pass the night."

No one's going to argue with that. Karalee flashes on the pastel pills as they appeared in the palm of her right hand, thinking, *Where have you been all my life?*

THE WOMAN DOES come eventually, bearing an old rubber box filled with bowls. She sets it down on the floor among them and immediately begins to pass the bowls around with accompanying spoons. "Better hurry up and eat. It's already melting."

Karalee peers down into her bowl. There are three scoops of ice cream of equal size, perfectly placed, sitting atop a bed of glistening sliced peaches.

"Oh, but wait," the woman says. "A final flourish." From the rubber box, she produces a battered metal pitcher. "Raspberry sauce. Wouldn't be peach melba without it."

Karalee watches the sauce coat the top of the ice cream and trickle down, nestling itself in among the peaches. Food photography op—if only she'd remembered to bring her camera!

"In the old days," the woman says wistfully, "I'd place a single fresh raspberry on top, I would. But the season for that is past."

"Not to worry," Gerard says, digging in.

"It's perfect," says Karalee. In the semidarkness and through her drug-induced haze, she watches the tip of her spoon disappear into the ice cream. When she was fifteen, she suffered from a bout of anorexia, which led to a year of psychotherapy that alleviated her worst symptoms but never fully rectified the accompanying OCD. Ever since then, dessert has always been the hardest meal for her, something she has to force herself to consume. But now her arm has a mind of its own, the spoon finding its way to her mouth. The treat hits her palate with a rush of sweetness, and she savors every drop, thinking that Chick was right, they'll have a story to tell from this. Who would've thunk it, as her mother likes to say. To have what amounts to a feast—here on an abandoned island.

Karalee thinks of Chick's boat, small waves lapping at it, swamped and looking pathetic among the riverside detritus of another age. Although the lights of Manhattan do still glaze the sky, their sources could be as far as the moon, for all the good they do. By rights, the Sewer Rats should be starving tonight for their collective stupidity.

They eat in silence, even the woman. She has joined them on the floor, sitting somewhat apart, her shabby skirt like a mountain of rags that she gathered around herself. Now, in the steady glow cast by the firelight, Karalee sees that it's exactly that, the woman's blouse and skirt are quilts of remnants, some pieces clearly cut from the striped mattress cloth and pillow lining they saw earlier, others gleaned from who knows where, probably from other utilitarian fabrics left behind at the abandoned hospital. One has to admire the self-sufficient practicality of it, Karalee thinks.

As she sets down her empty bowl, she once again registers the initial *S* near the top of her spoon handle, just like the one she saw on her borrowed dinner fork earlier. The woman notices her looking and raises her chin. "You're wondering about that, are you?"

"I saw the initial, and since I know this place was once called Riverside Hospital, it can't stand for that. Is it the first initial of your name?"

"Heavens no! I'm not fancy enough to have initials on my flatware. It's Slocum—the *General Slocum*. You've heard of that one?" She looks around at their faces and sees little recognition. "Time loses things. It was famous for its carnage once."

"It?" Gerard asks. "But you said he was a general."

"I don't know about him, why they named it after him, but they ruined his name with it, those who took it. In my time, it was a ship's name, not a person's. A big iron and wooden paddle steamer she was—handsome once, but they say she had seen better days by the time of the tragedy."

"What was the tragedy?" asks Chick.

"There's a story there, very sad to some. Happened right out here on the river."

"The East River?"

"And the shores of this island. Would you like to hear it?"

Karalee flashes on the amorphous figures that she saw in the dark among the collection of soot-coated things, and a pit of terror forms in her gut. In an instant, she decides that in fact she does not want to hear the story, but her friends clamor for it.

As they do so, the woman drinks Karalee in with her eyes. She must see that she's terrified, but Karalee attempts to mask her discomfort with an awkward smile. If this were a normal gathering around a campfire, she'd retreat to her tent to avoid the story. She fleetingly recalls without humor a mention earlier today of that great campfire tale: the Cropsey

Maniac. *Ho ho ho.* Hell. She is stuck. Just now she can't bear the thought of finding her way back to the ward alone in the dark. She clutches the barbecue fork that she used to roast the hot dogs.

"There's a curse lies over this place like a caul," the woman says, snarling, "carelessly put here by the men who owned the *General Slocum.*"

"They cursed the island?" Gerard asks, puzzled.

"Not through their words. Through their deeds. The *General Slocum,* as I said, was a paddle steamer. I don't know when she was first built or for what purpose, but by the time of the tragedy, she went out on pleasure cruises in the waters around Manhattan and Long Island."

"Like the Circle Line," Josh says.

"Don't know anything about that."

"It's a ferry for tourists. Painted green and red, I think, circumnavigates Manhattan."

The woman nods. "I may have seen something like that from time to time. The *General Slocum* was bigger, carried upwards of five thousand souls. In the library here, when there was a library, many newspaper articles gave the details. It took large charter parties on excursions all over, fed people dinner, entertained them. She was owned by the Knicker-bocker Steamship Company. They're the ones responsible."

"For the tragedy?" Estela asks.

"Ay." The woman tucks her chin. "For everything. The men who owned that company, they have blood on their hands, they do. On the fateful day of Wednesday, June 15, 1904—"

"What? 1904? That's a long time ago," Gerard notes. "Responsible or not, the owners would all be dead by now."

"Indeed. Along with them they killed. But the blood went unpaid." She rises to her feet, produces an iron poker from behind the boiler, tends the fire for a minute, and puts another log on. She sits back down, pulls at her skirt, and frowns. "On that day, the congregation of St. Mark's Evangelical Lutheran Church chartered the *General Slocum* for their annual rite of spring. Germans mostly. The church sat on the Lower East Side— the Little Germany district."

"Little Germany?" Josh says. "Where's that? I never heard of it."

"Is it not there any longer? It was once—I don't know the streets.

Many left after the tragedy, I heard. Couldn't stand the emptiness. They were Briehof's people, not mine."

Briehof, thinks Karalee. *I know that name. Common?* But no time to reflect just now, as the once-taciturn woman has begun burying them in words.

"In any event," she is saying, "they were mostly women and children aboard the ship that day. Churchgoing folks, as I said. Devout people who trusted God and trusted the rule makers. Fourteen hundred of them boarded the ship midmorning, sailing for Long Island Sound and a picnic luncheon they planned to take up Eatons Neck way, at a place called Locust Grove. But as she approached the area around Ninetieth Street in Manhattan, the ship caught fire."

Karalee recalls the emergency boats gathered at Hunts Point this morning. Smoke billowing into the sky. She hears the siren of the passing police cruiser, sees in her mind's eye a tarnished brass horn on a shelf in the hospital basement.

The wood inside the furnace crackles, and Karalee almost believes that the flames inside jump at the thoughts that just crossed her mind, a reminder of the destructive power of an uncontrolled blaze. She turns her attention back to the woman, whose face is lit by the light of the flames as never before. Her eyes, Karalee sees, are each a different color: one greenish and the other blue-gray. Her teeth are the unhealthy color of tobacco, but a full set. Her hair is a hedge of black with only a few gray strands. Her eyebrows are thick and expressive. They undulate as her gaze goes round the group.

"The fire started in the lamp room," the woman continues, "at about ten A.M. A boy saw it first—twelve-year-old boy who, like the crew, spoke German. He went to Captain Van Schaick. To tell him something was burning—or try to. The captain took it as a ruse, shooed the boy off."

"No way!" cries Estela.

"It's possible the boy was shy, didn't insist well enough. Could be he started the fire by playing with matches. Or one of his companions did. If so, the lad picked a bad place indeed. The fire spread quick, fed by the fuel of the lamp room. There was a crew of twenty-two on that ship, plus a dozen and a half other employees of the Knickerbocker Steamship Company." She spits out the name like an epithet. "They ran for the fire hoses but found them rotted. The hoses . . . they crumbled in their hands—useless. Could not conduct water from one end of the salon to the other, let alone all the way across the ship. She was a wooden structure above the hull, was the *General Slocum*. Few barriers stood in the fire's way."

She pauses, stares into the fire just in front of them: the fire in the boiler, crackling. "Captain Van Schaick, he saw it would not be doused so easy. He thought quick—or tried to. Gave orders to turn the ship and steer for the nearest pier in the Bronx. But the wind fed the fire, and she transformed into a full-blazing torch along the way. Some say the captain saw his crime writ larger still and flinched. He saw that she may have caused an inferno on the shore if she met anything flammable there."

Karalee thinks again of the fire at Hunts Point. She doesn't know what that area looked like eighty years ago, but she recalls seeing giant oil tanks off in that direction this morning. Imagine the scale, she thinks, of a shipborne fire so great that it presented a danger to structures on shore. She looks into the dancing furnace flames and shudders.

"Crime?" Chick asks.

"What?" The woman comes out of her storyteller's trance.

"You said the captain saw his crime."

"Ay. Listen, mister. With no means to stanch the fire, next the crew went for the lifeboats. They could not get them down. Not move them an inch. They'd been fixed to the decks and cabin walls with wire and sealed over with paint. Flammable paint. Heat blistering their necks and faces, no one could manage the effort required to free them boats. Defeated by flame and fatigue, they abandoned the effort."

"Minimal fire laws." Josh nods his head. "That was seven years before the Triangle Shirtwaist fire."

The woman stares with her mismatched eyes. "In my experience, laws exist to protect them in power, not immigrant women and children. What laws there were hardly mattered to Van Schaick and his lot anyway."

She takes a deep breath and lets it out slowly. "There were pictures in all the papers after. I can see them like it was yesterday. The *General Slocum* had three grand decks, and soon all three became engulfed. One deck soon collapsed onto the deck below." She snorts. "They were trapped on that boat like flies in a jar, most of them people. Surrounded by flames in whatever cabin area they occupied. Surrounded by water if they could make it to the rail. Few could swim to begin with. Others—you could call it panic or desperation. Lifeboats or no, they had to abandon that cursed ship. But in their haste, they jumped too close to the great paddles, which still churned. Those people got knocked unconscious, fell into the water, and drowned. Not that missing the paddles helped much. Under those circumstances, no ordinary passenger stood a chance."

The woman's gaze goes around the circle, pinning Karalee like a butterfly to a board.

"Think!"

The Sewer Rats startle. An hour ago, they'd have laughed at their own reaction. Now Karalee struggles to swallow, her tongue thick, her throat parched.

"Think what waters the *General Slocum* plied at that very moment. When them women, clutching their babes in their arms, jumped overboard in an attempt to save themselves, they dropped right into the current of Hell Gate. Hell Gate! In the grip of the powerful river, their heavy clothing—their corsets and dresses and petticoats—dragged them under." She shakes her head. "Drowned. So many of them. Helpless. Carried off like so much flotsam."

"How horrible!" Estela cries.

Karalee thinks of their discussion earlier in the day of the weavers in Cookstown. It was she herself—wasn't it?—who pointed out how the women's clothing became a liability around the looms. She looks down at her bare legs and shorts—the freedom she has today. It never would have occurred to a churchgoing woman in 1904 to immodestly strip off her dress in order to survive the river. For those women trying to save themselves and their children, their clothing became shackles. Did this occur to them as the weight of it dragged them to oblivion?

"Meanwhile," the woman continues, "Captain Van Schaick, having decided not to approach the Bronx shore proper, madly turned the ship around, calling for full steam ahead. She would make for the nearest bit of safety the captain could see—North Brother Island. Little did he know that this bloody island is no one's brother nor parent nor child. It is a pathetic orphan and always has been—an orphan that shelters no one without dire consequence. And as she headed for these shores in panic—facing a headwind, no less—the ship's motion through air fanned the flames worse than ever. Imagine something that size, lit up like a matchstick in the breeze. She would soon burn from bow to stern with such violence. . . ." Again the woman shakes her head. "One has to wonder whether the devil himself gave that captain his instructions."

She works her tongue in her mouth, the wet slapping sound reminding Karalee of meat hitting butcher block. "People were melting. Hot smoke scorched their lungs. Clothing and hair caught fire. Them lucky enough to remain yet untouched, the sweet sickly smell of burning flesh filled their nostrils. Friends, relatives, neighbors—rendered to tallow. And still a thousand yards till shore, every foot of progress producing another inch of flame. The safe zone shrinking every minute. Hundreds huddled on deck, pressed tighter and tighter together, screaming. Coughing on the smoke of burning flesh."

Karalee looks around. Her friends are riveted, aghast. She tries to put the basement room out of her mind for good, the images she saw there in the dark. May as well ask herself not to think of the vines that clothe every building here, the dampness and dust. May as well ask for the power to snap her fingers and transport them all back to Havermeyer.

The woman continues. "Some in utter desperation chose to toss their children into the river alone, in hopes by some miracle they could be rescued downstream. They grabbed what life preservers they could locate, hastily tied them onto the crying tots, said prayers, and dropped them overboard. Imagine them dangling over the side, clawing at their mothers' arms—don't let go, don't let go! Their very last moment on earth together consumed by terror. Imagine those mothers, hearts rent, final wet kisses, thinking: At least my child will be saved although I perish. But what was this? Peering over the rail, those mothers watched in despair as their flesh and blood bobbed once or twice in the water and then sank like stones. The life preservers were cheaply made with little regard to their most sober purpose. Some mothers, seeing this, dived into the water—now knowing full well they would join their children in death. In their hysteria, others ran headlong into the flames. And still others crumpled to the deck, despondent."

Estela has a hand to her mouth, her eyes as wide open as Karalee has ever seen them. Josh, his glasses removed, rubs his eyebrows. Chick stares into his own lap.

"Finally, after unfathomable minutes," says the woman, "the *General Slocum* smashed into the shore of North Brother. Staff and patients—having witnessed the carnage from afar—raced to the ship's aid, but they were ill equipped, and the heat of the flames kept most from approaching too close. It was the nurses took over—the nurses used to finding their purpose while others rushed helplessly about. They organized a human chain, pulling the luckiest from the water at one end and working them inland for medical attention at the other."

Karalee peers through the boiler house window at the moonlit plaza area beyond, now largely filled in by trees. She imagines it as it once must have appeared, open lawns meant for strolling where people witnessing the *Slocum* disaster shouted in panic, banding together to face the horror of burned survivors. Those survivors no doubt suddenly grateful for the presence of disease carriers whom they would have shunned an hour before.

"Most of the passengers—them who lived till the moment of crash landing—were left to their own devices," says the woman, "abandoned to their own fate. For hours, their wails could be heard echoing from one end of North Brother to the other. Them choking. Them burning. Them drowning. And them who collapsed in shock and despair."

Karalee lets out a sigh, feeling the utter hopelessness of it.

The woman stares in her direction. "Unjust. That's the word. Some smaller boats—those that were on the river—raced to the island by the dozen. A few came to help—for what little help they could offer. Others ferried men who went up and down the shore removing jewelry from the bodies that washed up, emptying their pockets of valuables."

"Scavengers!" Gerard says. "They must have been arrested, right?"

"Ay, a few, I suppose. Not many. There were too many other things to do. It was summer, remember. The water warm. The sun out in force. Those bodies would soon cause a stench."

"What did they do with the corpses?" Josh asks.

"Returned them to their next of kin, those they could identify, and eventually buried in Brooklyn and Queens. 'Earth's purest children, young and fair.' More than a thousand souls slipped their sorry flesh that day, crying with their last breaths for retribution. Which they never got on earth, by the way. The Knickerbocker Steamship Company paid a small fine. The captain, blinded in one eye by a flying ember but otherwise unscathed, served little more than three years in prison for the crime of criminal negligence. Negligence indeed! Careless murder, more like."

Karalee closes her eyes, shakes her head. In her mind, she sees the sign from the basement among the other relics of the *General Slocum* disaster. GENTLEMA—the men's room. But she saw no sign for the women's. Perhaps that one was completely consumed by fire or sank with other bits of wreckage to the bottom of the deep river.

THEY SIT FOR a long time in silence, the fire in the furnace dying. Finally, Chick jumps up and rekindles it with more logs. Thick ash, receiving the logs, muffles what sound the crashing firewood makes. And in the wake of the dramatic story—related almost with the emotion of an eyewitness—a hush lies so heavily upon everything that Karalee startles when the woman speaks again, ticking off on her mannish fingers.

"Briehof's aunt on his mother's side, his married sister, his niece, and his young nephew were aboard that ship. No grown men accompanied them. One spinster cousin was the only survivor in his small family."

Josh turns to her, puzzled. "Who's Briehof?"

The woman doesn't respond. She looks into the fire, which has sprung back to life.

"Who's Briehof?" Josh wants to know more insistently.

Karalee remembers now. She nudges him with her elbow.

The woman, whose energy has settled inward, ignores his inquiry again. When Josh opens his mouth to ask a third time, Karalee jabs him harder to keep him quiet. He winces and finally takes the hint. The woman rises to her feet, wiping her hands on her skirt. "Many nights," she says, "I hear the cries of the German women and children in—in my sleep. They cry in physical pain, but also in another kind of pain— the torture of eternal injustice."

No one stirs.

"How sad," Estela says quietly. "Thank you for sharing their story."

"Ay." A moment ago the woman stood, barely noticed, and has been drifting to the door. She stops abruptly. "Until today," she says, "it has been a long time since anyone thanked me for anything."

Chick pushes himself to his feet and takes a step in her direction with his hand extended for a shake. Her stare brings him up short, and he drops the hand back to his side, slides it into his pocket. "You've been kind to us tonight." He scratches the stubble on his cheek with the fingers of his left hand. "But we don't even know your name."

"All my talking, I neglected that, did I?" She cocks her head, lifts an eyebrow. "Well, I suppose there's no harm. It's Mary. That's my name."

They express their gratitude all around. "Will we see you in the morning?" Gerard asks.

"I don't know," Mary admits. "I don't keep such regular hours."

"Well, if we're gone when you wake up—"

"Then I'll not trouble myself."

Mary

For the first time in a long while, the ghosts do not harry Mary as she moves through the dark on her nightly walk around the island. Their cries begin far off and never approach, and no vision accompanies them.

Not a peep from Mathilde either, although Mary felt her over her shoulder back at the boiler house.

The intruders' boat is well scuttled, dragged out a few feet by the force of the river but no farther, held to the shore by its anchor. She stares at the cloudy water inside it for a time, and the sight reminds her of the *General Slocum*, which settled on a nearby shoal, hollowed out but with its iron hull intact. Someone later repurposed that hull for a barge, the medical supply clerk, Mr. Cunningham, told her once. Not many years after that, it sank for good in a storm off Long Island. That was the eighth and final incident surrounding the ship, which was doomed as North Brother Island is doomed.

As Mary is doomed.

Bringers of calamity all.

And what she does not say—cannot admit to herself—is that deep down, she understands what drove Captain Van Schaick away from all admission of responsibility for those he killed through his negligence. For to allow one drop of sympathy into his heart would be to open the floodgates and to drown himself in that very sympathy.

What riles her, however, is not what she has in common with the captain but what makes them different. Van Schaick, who had infamy thrust upon him in his day, ended up pardoned by the President of the United States. Mary, made infamous forever, was left to rot on the very island where Van Schaick's victims breathed their last—more victims in number than she ever killed by a factor of one hundred.

Out in the middle of the river, a tugboat passes, rumbling like a small earthquake, a single floodlight cutting through the darkness. Its beam does not venture in her direction. The crew knows what lies here.

Captain Van Schaick, she recalls, abandoned ship via tugboat. Unruffled, some say. As brave, thinks Mary, as George A. Soper when confronted by her carving fork.

The only man in her life that she ever saw brave was the judge who briefly freed her, standing up to public opinion. He made her promise never to cook again, and out of respect she obeyed for a little while. But when long hot days in the laundry and Briehof's bottomless laziness reduced their household resources to nothing more than a few pennies, she took up the only lucrative work she knew, and damn the consequences.

To this day, she does not know precisely how many people died by her actions—by her hand, she supposes one could say. Far fewer than by the hands of those responsible for the deaths of Mathilde and Friede and little tiny Adolf, that is for sure. She views Van Schaick's body count versus hers as an imbalance in the human ledger. An imbalance requiring correction. And, although she was never much good at maths, in any reasonable accounting there must be some additional factoring for a long stretch of time without justice. In any case, five more, by her calculus, will only be a start.

But a start it will be.

Life stretches out before her as it always has, a waiting game with moments that clutch at her but never seem to guide her anywhere. Has her whole life not been consumed by waiting? Waiting for things to improve? Waiting for the men to come and assert their will against her? Waiting for ever-elusive death, which once refused to take her by means of typhoid and continues to avoid her with a kind of passive malice? For she has been exposed to nearly every pathogen on earth with no ill effect.

Her hands, from a lifetime at the hearth, are impervious to pain. A fall down the stairs once left her with little more than a few fleeting bruises. Even the infirmities of age began some years ago to keep their distance from Mary.

Which has its benefits. She can wield an ax better than an ordinary man.

Completing her examination of the Soper girl's boat, she is sure that it will rescue no one tonight. In that case, allow time to do its work. Like the fertilized eggs of the night heron she sometimes eats. Like the wearing down of her cottage to a pile of sticks by weather. Like the spoiled brats and imperious ladies her cooking eventually made to suffer and die.

An incubation period, Soper called it.

Incubation, indeed. With that word swimming in her mind, she walks along slowly, heavily, but at peace. Back to the heart of her prison.

Karalee

CHICK'S CANDLE GUTTERED to uselessness an hour ago in the drafty ward upstairs. Standing in darkness, Gerard watches from a window as Mary turns the corner of a crumbling building in the faint remaining moonlight.

"I wonder where she's going. You think Mary's her real name?"

"Could be," says Chick. "It's a common enough name."

"Maybe," Estela says, "she heard the Typhoid Mary story and took the name in sisterhood, in solidarity."

"Right," says Chick. "Because it's so cool to associate yourself with a mass murderer."

"Why not? The punks would do that, I bet. Kind of like the Dead Kennedys."

"Did that babbling woman look like a punk rocker to you?"

"Far from babbling," Josh says, "I thought she spit out a great story. A little heavy on the macabre, what with all those people consumed by fire and drowning and so on, but far from incoherent." He turns to Karalee. "Why did you poke me when I asked her about that guy she mentioned?"

"Briehof. A name you should know."

"*Moi?*"

"Since you're Mr. Know-It-All."

"Help me out. It has to do with public health? New York? The ten plagues of Egypt? Gimme a hint."

"When she was talking, I remembered something we all forgot earlier. I couldn't ask her to clarify—not then. But Typhoid Mary's companion ... his name was Briehof."

"Of course!"

"Don't pretend to be remembering now," teases Estela.

"They lived together when she wasn't on the job," Karalee says. "He's the guy—"

"Right! The guy who your great-grandfather bribed with drink to give up the goods on Mary Mallon."

"Another upstanding citizen," Chick mutters.

"Would you give it a rest, Chick!"

"Wait a minute," Gerard says, lighting up a couple of joints and passing them around. "She was talking like she knew this Briehof guy personally. She said those were his people on the ship. That most of his family died in the accident."

"It wasn't an accident," Karalee says. "If the story's true as she told it, that was complete disregard for the safety of those passengers."

"The story of the *General Slocum* is true enough," Josh says. "When she was talking, I remembered that there's a monument to it in Tompkins Square Park in Alphabet City. The junkies pitch their tents beside it."

"You've been there?" Gerard asks.

"High school, but not for heroin ... just walking around. Anyway, I did some reading on this in an undergraduate history course. The *Slocum* disaster was in fact exacerbated by negligence, no question. But placing blame didn't prove so easy. Fire laws and shipping regulations were much looser at the time."

Estela is rubbing her temples with her fingers, as if to massage out an idea. "The way that woman phrased things ... I thought it was a little strange. Like she was there at the time or something. She used the phrase 'in my time' or 'in my day.' Something like that."

Josh's jaw drops open. "What are we saying? That woman is Typhoid Mary? And she just cooked us dinner? I think I'm gonna heave."

"Whoa! If you act any more paranoid," Chick says, "I'm banning you from more pot."

"Too late," says Gerard. "Those two joints were the last of it."

"If she were alive," Karalee calmly points out, "Typhoid Mary would now be a hundred and thirteen years old. The homeless woman looked middle-aged, no more than fifty."

"So she's delusional," Gerard says. "However she came to this island, she knew the history and absorbed it as her own. She's taken on the persona of Typhoid Mary. I bet our boat didn't get wrecked in an accident. That woman scuttled it."

Chick holds up a palm. "Keep your shorts on, Gerry. Why would she do such a thing?"

"Pure malice. Why did she keep spreading all that disease back in the day?"

"Because that was a different person, dude. I'm starting to wonder how I gave each of you people an A in my class. I reiterate what Karalee said. If Typhoid Mary were alive today, she would be one of the oldest people on earth."

Josh holds up a finger. "But it's not outside the realm of biological possibility."

"And she wouldn't have a full head of dark hair."

"She dyes it," Gerard suggests.

"Oh, right. With the Clairol she buys at the North Brother A&P. And another thing to consider while you're concocting crazy theories: At more than a hundred years old, she wouldn't have the capability of smashing up a boat. Would she? As a matter of fact, few women of any age would have the strength to do that."

"Did you see the hands on her, the way she walks?"

"Yeah, because that's a much younger woman, not Typhoid Mary. Who's dead, anyway. And the homeless woman has no cause to shipwreck us. I fucked up by running the *Fledge* aground, an honest mistake. Now would you guys quit queering my high? There's only a few hours till daylight. Before you know it, we'll be sober."

"And face the sober reality that we're stuck on this island with a madwoman." Josh groans.

"No. And face the reality that we need to fix the boat or get ourselves rescued."

"A distinction without a difference."

"Oh, please. Point is there's nothing for us to do tonight. Nothing to—" He waves his hands. "—work out." Spinning around. "You've grown awful quiet, Kiki. You tired? You ready to bed down?"

"Not with you, Chick." She doesn't disagree with his analysis of the homeless woman, but in other respects she has lost all patience with him.

"Oh." He puts a hand to his heart. "I am cut. Is it over between us, just like that?"

"We're in no condition to have this discussion."

"Well, there's only four cots and there are five of us. Maybe someone else wants to keep the professor warm. Not you, Gerard. I'm not that kind of guy. Estela, how about you, babe?"

"You're a pig, Chick." It sounds like *peeg* when she says it. "I'll share with Josh." She walks over and puts an arm around him, and Josh embraces her with the disbelieving tentativeness of the newly blessed.

The tender moment lasts a beat until they hear a scream outside—a scream so grating that it penetrates to the bone marrow. There's no telling exactly where it comes from, but in her mind's eye, Karalee flashes on the open throat of a tortured child.

THE MOMENT HANGS in the air. Around them, the room looks grayer.

"What was that? What the hell was that?" Gerard says. "Mary?"

"More like a kid." Chick shakes his head. "What am I saying? Probably a wild bird of some kind. Maybe a screech owl."

"In the middle of Manhattan?"

"We're not in the middle of Manhattan. This is a bird sanctuary, remember? Which probably explains all the looniness."

"Ha. Ha."

They hear it again. More than one voice this time. Karalee feels it in the pit of her intestines. Before she can process it further, an entire chorus pipes in.

Gerard runs to the window again and peers out. "They must be out there somewhere, but I don't see anything." He backs away from the window and doesn't turn around until he's within a foot of the cots. "What do we do about this?"

"We do nothing," Chick argues. "The sounds are out there and we're in here. We can congratulate ourselves on not choosing to camp in the woods tonight."

The voices are taking on the texture of Gregorian chant, but without any consistent tone or rhythm. They echo as if escaping from the open doors of a cathedral or a monastery, but Karalee feels eerily that these voices are escaping from an otherworldly chamber. Her mind leaps again to the basement storage room, among what she now knows to be the salvaged objects of the doomed ship—an *S* on each piece of cutlery. Did she hear a similar sound down there, if only for a moment? She thinks of Mary's references to the cries of German mothers and children whose tortured souls, if trapped on earth, might very well have good reason to cry out. In fact, a part of her believes that's the only explanation that makes sense. Yet another part thinks birds—and on second thought, she'd much rather birds. She can't bring herself to mention the *General Slocum* to anyone just now.

Josh lets out a moan and, in a fit of manic action, dumps one mattress and pillow on the floor and rapidly slides the empty cot frame across the floor to the open doorway with a crash. He flips it over on its side, legs facing into the room, rusty springs twanging.

"What good's that gonna do?" Chick asks him.

Josh pulls the frame forward a few inches, as it would move if pushed from outside, and the sharp edges of the tube legs, long missing their feet, make a scraping sound across the floor. "This way, at least we'll hear them coming," he says, pushing the frame flush with the doorframe again.

Chick throws a thumb toward the window. "If they wanted to sneak up on us—whoever *they* are—they're not making a very good show of it."

"So no one thinks they're birds?" Karalee asks desperately.

Josh adjusts the glasses on his nose. Chick and Gerard rest their hands on their hips and look at her incredulously.

"I'd rather," says Estela, hugging herself, "they keep up the racket. So long as they do, we know they're still out there and not inside."

Karalee picks up her camera—she lost its case somewhere along the way—and wills herself to the window. The voices are no louder from here, but they persist, overlapping one another, reverberating. She lifts the viewfinder to her eye and peers out through the dirty glass panes into the relic of the old plaza, dimly lit by a fading moon. Nothing moves below. Nothing but the half-dead leaves of early autumn trees, shifting in a light breeze. Suddenly the scar on her left ear itches, and she claws at it, almost in anger. No further sign of Mary out there, the woman who knows this island best. They were unafraid in her matronly presence, at least once they'd identified her as harmless. Now Karalee, isolated with her closest friends, feels more uneasy than she has all night. They are out of their realm. They don't belong here.

She closes her eyes, struggles for a deep breath in the stale air. *I am stoned*, she acknowledges to herself. She is well aware, as the voices wash over her in waves, that she ingested more mind-altering substances in the past eight hours than she has consumed in a lifetime. And yet, all the Sewer Rats hear these sounds, not just her.

They decide to huddle on the cots—what safer place than bed, they've been trained since childhood—but with the fourth cot against the door-frame, they're now down to three usable ones. Karalee spins on her heels. "I'll share a bed with Gerard."

She sets her camera down on the nearest mattress, and without another word, they push all three cots closer together, circling the wagons.

As he joins her on the cot, Gerard mumbles something.

"What?" Karalee says. "Speak up."

"I wish we'd thought to gather up some food from the pantry before coming up here. We'll have the munchies soon."

"You can eat at a time like this?"

He shrugs. "It's all this weightlifting. I'm constantly famished."

"You'll have to wait until morning. It's dark now and there's nothing to light the way. And——" She jabs her thumb toward the window, as Chick did a moment ago.

"I know." Gerard clasps his hands together and lets a visible shiver run through him. Starvation? Fear? "How do you want to do this?" He sighs and pats the narrow mattress. "This bicycle wasn't built for two."

Karalee has no strength to wrap her mind around the geometry. She doesn't want to use the mattress from the overturned cot—no one does; it would put them too close to the floor. Nor is Chick's bed an option she wishes to consider any longer. But she doesn't like the idea of spooning with Gerard either—would prefer not to be touched by anyone just now. Her eyes feel heavy from the drugs and the long day. She hands Gerard the pillow that landed on the floor when Josh overturned the cot and curls into a ball at the foot of the bed with her head on the other pillow.

Outside, the unsettling chorus drones on, and she can't help listening. She won't move an inch, but it keeps her awake for a long time. Keeps them all awake; she senses it. The cries outside almost fade to silence for a while; then they rise again with renewed volume, continually changing in pitch and tone. As if someone were twisting the knob back and forth on an amplifier.

Karalee begins to make out spoken syllables among the moaning. Then they come again.

"Did anyone hear that?"

"Jesus Christ," Josh says.

At once they all run to the window, staying close together—close friends—the Sewer Rats gang.

"They're words, all right," says Chick. "Or fragments of words. This can't be happening." He runs a hand through his hair, scratches the stubble on his cheek.

"Can anyone make them out?" Gerard asks.

They shake their heads. The words, Karalee thinks, have a raspy texture, communicating anxiety. Sometimes they sound like English and other times like German, but they never achieve full articulation. Like dream words that die in the throat without breaking through to the conscious world.

After listening for a while, they retreat back to their cots, their anxiety thick but becoming familiar. Karalee's head feels heavy, as if the sounds cast a sleeping spell over her. One moment her chin is falling and the next she sits up, terrified, with the silence of her friends around her only adding to her torment—the weighty absence of their familiar joking around and theorizing. Without saying a word—perhaps by that very act—they have receded into their own private worlds, alone with their thoughts in this eerie place under these strange circumstances.

Karalee, when she is half awake—as opposed to half asleep—tries to posit any number of explanations for the disturbing cries outside: birds or other creatures, the wind moving through empty buildings, the sounds of passing boat motors distorted by the river. Yet deep down, she knows the noises come from none of those things. The word fragments, when she discerns them, belie all innocent theories. It is the sound of agony, trapped in a netherworld while desperately seeking expression in this one.

The voices—they are surely voices—erupt and recede. They flutter up and die down again. Now and then, silence finally appears to have settled upon the island. But soon the wailing rises once more, like a gaggle of geese exhorting one another. She wonders if she will ever sleep tonight. She fears sleep—especially fears the prospect of having a nightmare in this place. But at the same time, she knows that sleep would provide welcome relief from the unsettling racket of the *General Slocum*'s souls.

Her chin drifts down again. She is profoundly tired. After some time, her eyelids become so heavy that the mercy of sleep proves irresistible. Her nostrils have grown accustomed to the smell of the musty pillow that she hugs like a life preserver. Her fetal position protects her as much as a body can. Her head lolls and she sleeps deeply and does not fall into the trap of a nightmare. Some time later, for a few brief moments she drifts back up to consciousness and half opens her eyes. In washed-out darkness, Gerard stands at the window, looking out. He is contemplative, not panicked. She wants to tell him to return to bed, but though they share a cot, they're not really sleeping together, so the impulse seems out of place. In any case, she remains frozen with fatigue. Her heavy eyelids close fast again, and the cries that undulate outside, now almost familiar, tempt her back to sleep like the notes of a deranged lullaby.

A DAMP CHILL reaches Karalee, and she clenches into a tighter ball to fend it off. Morning has broken, and early daylight penetrates the ward, but not harshly. There are no direct rays of sun.

She sits up, groggy and sandy-eyed. She senses movement around her, the whole gang stirring. Chick, on the cot behind her, lets out a groan as he stretches. Josh and Estela are purring at one another. Karalee extends her arm along the mattress.

"Where's Gerard?" She twists around.

"Dunno," Chick says. "Off to use the facilities? Morning constitutional?"

She recalls seeing him last night standing by the window, as if the ethereal voices entranced him. "Did anyone see him leave?"

"Uh-uh."

"No."

"I'll look," Josh says. In the freshness of morning, he seems unintimidated. Everything around them feels less threatening. And why shouldn't it? They were only noises. He swings the overturned cot out of the way and pops out into the hall, returning a minute later, adjusting the glasses on his nose with a pinky. "He must have gone all the way outside."

"Well, shit," Chick says. "Nice of him to tell us."

"Maybe he didn't want to wake you, Professor."

"Like I even slept a wink with that maniacal yowling outside." He pauses. "At least it's gone quiet."

"If you didn't sleep a wink," Karalee says, "you should've seen Gerard leave."

"Don't tax me this early, woman. Am I my brother's keeper?"

Karalee runs her tongue around her desiccated mouth. She'd give over her worldly possessions for a toothbrush. "What's our next move?"

"We raid the pantry one more time, round up our Korean friend, make a plan of escape."

"And blow this Pepsico stand," Estela concludes.

"It's 'popsicle stand,'" Josh gently corrects, taking her hand.

They find their way down to the kitchen again, so few signs of their presence last night that Karalee almost wonders whether the dinner party was all a hallucination. But Josh discovers a smooth disk of dried wax in the middle of the cafeteria table. He scrapes it up with a fingernail and rolls it into a ball, which he tosses across the room. It pats dully into the crumbled detritus at the base of a wall.

Sunlight filters through a set of windows on the east side of the building. In fresh light, the place looks filthier than ever. On the floor and cafeteria furniture, written in the thick dust, they see indications of every step they took and every brush across a countertop with a stray elbow. There are also the footprints of large bare feet.

Chick steps around their old food cooler, which lies open and empty on its side in a puddle of water, and pulls open the pantry door. Full boxes and dented unopened cans litter the floor, as if thrown aside in a feverish rush. He cocks his head. One shelf has a gaping breach in its contents, the label of a large can toward the back barely legible: peaches in syrup.

They gulp warm soda and chew saltines and butter cookies. This time the joy of discovery has worn off, as well as any concern about the food's condition. To Karalee, it's just fuel. She eats greedily.

Chick suppresses a belch and steps into the hallway, bellowing. "Gerard! Gerard! Gerry!" The others join in, cupping their mouths and facing all four directions. "Gerard!"

No answer comes, but they are more annoyed than worried. It's a big building, and their voices don't carry far. "I'm tempted to leave that bastard behind," Chick says, not meaning it.

He finds a box of matches on a shelf and attempts to light the stove, but fails. "How'd she do it for the stew? The thing doesn't even smell of gas." He flicks the burnt-out match across the kitchen. "And what about the bread? How do you suppose she baked that?" Attempting to answer his own question, he opens one large oven door to reveal a hive of white maggots writhing in cold grease. "Aw! God!" He lets the door spring back with a clatter and recoils from the cooking area without touching another thing.

Meanwhile, Josh begins poking around an unexplored corner or two. "She is genuinely disgusting, and we ate her cooking," he says, swallowing hard. "Check this out."

Green bottle flies buzz in circles around their heads. Chick swats at them in futility.

Karalee and the others approach to see what Josh is looking at. They find themselves standing over a small closet with the broken door jammed open, the inside of the closet piled three feet high with the filthy shards of smashed dishes—those from last night resting on top.

As the four of them, shoulder to shoulder, stare into the mess, contemplating, Karalee thinks perhaps she sees one of the shards move. At first she doubts it could be, and then all at once she becomes sure of it. The shard scrapes against the broken edge of another plate and settles six inches below with a ping. A jet-black snout, whiskers, and red beady eyes reveal themselves, looking less startled than they ought to be. Then another and another and another rat appears. Karalee's face twitches back in disgust while Estela screams and the men yelp. With Estela in the lead, they all set off running—away from the closet, across the kitchen, through the cafeteria, into the atrium, and out the front door. Karalee has never seen Estela move so fast.

In the plaza, spinning around, scanning, seeing no more rats and beginning to feel safe, they double over laughing at the absurdity of their own reaction.

The day has dawned bright and crisp outside, with cirrus clouds and contrails splashed against a clear blue sky. Karalee sucks a deep breath of fresh air and feels better.

When Chick stops laughing, he says, "Did you see the look on Josh's face?"

"Man!" Josh shakes his head. "I'm not ashamed to admit that scared the crap out of me. Uhhhhggh." He shudders.

"And *we're* supposed to be the Sewer Rats!" Chick guffaws. "Those were our cousins!"

When they've laughed themselves into composure, Estela asks, "So what about Gerard? Do we split up to find him?"

"No." Chuck twists his jaw, thinking it over. "We stick together."

"Maybe he got up early," Josh theorizes. "Went off to get a head start on fixing the boat."

"I'm sure you're right," Karalee chimes in, though she's not at all sure. "He's back at the *Fledge* waiting for us."

They decide to head north around the Tuberculosis Pavilion, calling for him as they go. That way, if he's inside the building, he might hear their voices through a window. From there, they'll swing around to the eastern shore. If he's not at the boat, they'll go back the way they came when they arrived yesterday, comb through the other buildings.

"Gerard! Gerard!" Their voices echo off the ruins of the once-grand pavilion. "Gerard! Gerard!"

Estela's voice has grown thin and reedy, lost all its piquancy. "He's at the *Fledge.* Has to be at the *Fledge.*" She's convincing herself. Inside, she must suspect what Karalee does: that Gerard went off on a foolish adventure, one that will waste their time when they need to turn all their attention to planning an escape or effecting a rescue.

No answer comes from the vicinity of the pavilion.

With Josh in the lead, they plunge into the woods, calling out every few steps, their voices skipping across the exposed schist. Before long, they have neared the river again. When they are close enough to see the gray water through the trees, the sound of a motorboat drifts to them.

"Maybe he's got her started," Josh says.

"But I have the key," says Chick.

They wear half smiles on their faces, however, smiles that say, *That clever Gerard. He hot-wired the boat somehow.* Karalee, wanting to believe, imagines him standing bare chested at the wheel, bow pointed homeward, peering over his shoulder with a goofy smile on his own face. Maybe he even wears his Padres cap again. She reaches for her camera as they clamber across roots and ground-hugging vines to the shore. But Gerard isn't there. Only the swamped boat, rocking in the current.

A big barge hauling a mountain of gravel with cranes poised over its midships like inverted fishing hooks slides silently up the middle of the river, a snub-nosed tugboat strapped alongside. Upon spotting it, Josh and Chick scramble up to the small rise at the edge of the woods and jump up and down, waving their arms and screaming for help, but their voices don't even seem to leave the riverbank. It is futile, Karalee knows. They can't even hear the motor from the tug at this distance, which means for certain the tug can't hear them.

When the barge has fully passed, Josh and Chick climb back down. "I have an idea," Chick says, wading out to the *Flagellum*. He explains that he can use the outboard motor as a bilge pump, substantially empty the boat of water—if only temporarily—and assess the damage. He climbs aboard and inserts the key. The motor grinds away, but won't turn over. Chick fiddles with the primer and tries again with the same result. He looks down into the water, which has a rainbow slick floating on it— traces of lost gasoline. He stands with his hands clasped under his pony- tail and stares out at the horizon.

"It's all right. We don't need gas, actually. The river current is our fuel. We just need her to float." He seems to have forgotten that his main purpose was to pump the boat dry with the motor, not to use it for pro- pulsion just now. "If we can tip her over on her side," he explains, "we'll see where the damage is."

"A regular Robinson Crusoe," Josh mutters.

Chick fixes him with a stare out the corner of one eye. "You got a better idea, Jewboy?"

Josh's jaw stiffens. "No, Professor Hitler."

"Then let's do this."

He climbs down, and they space out every three feet along the port side with Chick at the stern and the women in the middle, Estela even gamely attempting to use her bad arm a little. With Chick calling the shots, between effortful grunts they rock the *Flagellum* up and down, water sloshing inside and out, but they can't come close to turning her over.

After five minutes, they collapse back on shore, sweating, gasping. Chick has his face in his hands. "Fucking Gerard!" he explodes. "Wan- dering off. Where is that guy when you need him? We were this close!"

"You're kidding," Josh says without humor. "We have as much chance of flipping that boat over with our bare hands as—"

"Shut the hell up, Joshua." It is Estela. "You're being negative."

"We're stranded."

"We'll think of something. Chick will think of something."

Chick. Karalee has never seen him under the shadow of despair before. He sits on the sand with his head between his knees, facing east with the sun on his right cheek, his focus concentrated on the place where the river slaps against the crumbling seawall. She should go to him, encourage him. They will need his strength. But she can't bring herself to approach after the way he's treated everybody. Instead, she picks up her camera and takes his picture. But her heart isn't even in that. She sets the camera aside and they all sit for a while, gathering strength for their next move.

ESTELA IS THE first one up, leaning on Josh's shoulder to get to her feet. "We stop wasting time now. The *Fledge* is a lost cause. First we need to find Gerard."

"Agreed," Karalee says.

"We're not the Sewer Rats without him," says Josh.

They trudge through the woods again with Estela in the lead, eventually coming upon the small clearing with the chopping block. The ax is there, its blade buried in the stump. Chick walks up and rests a hand on the handle. "Anyone remember how I left this the last time we came through here?" It seems like ages ago. They shake their heads, shrug, and move along.

This time, when they emerge from the woods into the remnants of the plaza, they head south to the greenhouse. Someone there moves among the planting beds. Karalee's heart lifts and they all pick up their pace. But then they see it's only the vagabond, Mary, tending her garden on hands and knees.

She lifts her face when they get close enough. "Good day."

A ray of sun passes through a pane of greenhouse glass, casting a prismatic spectrum on the footing of a cinder block wall.

"It's a beautiful day," Estela chirps, "except we lost our friend Gerard. Have you seen him?"

Mary is sucking the marrow from a bone. Using her tongue, she steers it from one corner of her mouth to another. She frowns and thrusts out her lower lip, shakes her head. "I sure haven't. Maybe he wanted some privacy."

Karalee doesn't suppose any elaboration will come from Mary. She wants to ask about the disturbing voices last night, but when her gaze locks with the older woman's, she freezes. In daylight, it could not be more clear that one eye is blue and the other is green. "Can I take your picture?" she asks on impulse.

A smile forms, showing Mary's snail-shell teeth. "If you'll be quick, girl." She works the bone round her mouth. "I've work to do." She gets to her feet and wipes her hands together to dislodge most of the soil, making no effort to clean it all off. She raises her chin proudly as Kara-lee rests a finger on the shutter of her camera. Through the viewfinder, Karalee notices a bad shadow occluding half her subject's face. She lowers the camera to assess with her naked eye, but the shadow has gone away. Maybe her finger got into the frame, but that's not like her—she's more experienced than that. When she looks again, the shadow remains. Odd. She snaps the photo anyway.

"Thank you."

"We better keep moving," Josh says. "Gerard, you know." He holds up his hands.

"I'm sure you will find him soon," says Mary. "We're confined here. He can't have gotten far." She looks down at Chick's legs. They dried on the walk, but pasted down with river water, the hair has matted in a swirly pattern. "How is your boat, lad?"

"Oh, just dandy."

"*Flagellum*, right? What might that mean?"

Chick replies pedagogically without thinking. "A flagellum is the whiplike appendage of a one-celled animal, used for locomotion." Then surprise crosses his face. "You've been to her?"

Mary nods. "I took a walk this morning."

"Then you know it's a project. Are there any tools around?"

"Ay. A few." Her gaze falls to a trowel resting on the greenhouse frame.

"Not what I had in mind," Chick grumbles.

They resume walking, and as soon as Mary's out of sight, they begin calling for Gerard again, returning to the Tuberculosis Pavilion and the gymnasium. At the boiler house, Karalee finds her barbecue fork lying in the dust. She picks it up and slides the handle into the waistband at the back of her shorts with the tines pointing up. Having possession of it again makes her feel better about their prospects, for some reason, gives her confidence that they'll get out of this mess before long.

They work their way to the remnants of the old pier and look up and down the small beach as best they can, especially concentrating on the view south past the foghorn tower with its bent lightning rod, near which the ruins of several smaller unexplored buildings huddle. A thread of desperation has begun to creep into their voices as they continue to call for Gerard. They have covered a lot of territory, consumed the better part of two hours.

No one articulates the thought that crept into Karalee's mind some time ago and now churns relentlessly. That Gerard followed the sound of the voices last night. That the German banshees—or whatever they are—might have carried him to their netherworld or—less fantastically—tempted him straight into the river, where even a grown man could easily drown in the strong current.

She tells herself to stop letting her imagination run wild, that it won't help anything. And sure enough, as they approach the lighthouse area, they spot on the piled riprap boulders below it the salmon-colored T-shirt they know Gerard was wearing last night.

Estela is the first to speak. "It's him!" she gasps with pleasure, all the beauty returning to her face.

Chick cups his hands around his mouth and bellows. "Gerard, you asshole!"

If they follow the shore, the ruins of the old lighthouse building will block their view. They find an alternative approach in the remnants of a footpath that passes through a collapsed fence, wending among dense trees. The salmon T-shirt moves—they all see it—and they break into smiles, picking up their pace, calling out to Gerard, who doesn't answer. He is lying on his back, Karalee now determines, and appears to be sunbathing. Maybe he fell asleep. And now she notices that there is someone with him, a person wearing white, maybe sitting beside him. She chuckles to herself, could stick her barbecue fork under his chin for all the anxiety he's caused them this morning, but decides she'll give him a big kiss when she gets there instead. And that person sitting beside him, wherever he came from, has the makings of their savior.

But something doesn't fit. Josh sees it first. "That's a bird. It's a bird." He begins to jog, and Chick follows in close formation.

Knowing that Estela can't move fast over uneven ground, Karalee is torn. Not wanting to leave her behind, she follows the men at a middling pace, keeping Estela in sight with frequent glances back over her shoulder. She pauses to reach out a hand and help Estela over a fallen tree, then stretches a bit of a lead ahead of her again.

When Josh gets within fifteen yards of Gerard, the bird spreads its wings, hops twice, and takes off. At that moment, Karalee realizes that the creature was sitting on Gerard's chest. A great big seagull, gray and white. It now hovers in the air twenty feet above him, crying out. *Keow! Keow!*

Just as Josh reaches Gerard, the seagull flies off in a widening gyre, soaring above the gable that Karalee first spotted when she identified the island. It disappears into the clear sky.

Josh is kneeling beside Gerard as Chick reaches him. Then Chick also falls to his knees on the craggy breakwater boulders. They have their hands resting on Gerard's chest and right leg as Karalee catches up. She can't understand what she's seeing. He was sunbathing, right? Was he feeding that bird? Maybe offering it some crackers from the pantry?

Behind her, Estela has begun muttering something she can't understand. "His size. His size." What is she going on about? What size? Karalee snaps her head around.

Estela's face has crumpled into a rictus of sorrow, her palm covering her mouth, her fingernails digging into her cheeks so hard it looks like she'll rip the skin open.

"His eyes," she's saying. Not *his size.* "His eyes."

Karalee spins back around and finally sees what Estela sees. Where Gerard's eyes should be, there are two gaping craters of bloody jelly.

Mary

She has caught another rabbit with the snare. When the Soper girl and her friends walk away, draped in uncertainty, Mary spits out her bone and goes to fetch the carcass.

Mathilde is there. "What happened to the Chinaman?"

"Don't pretend you didn't see. I suppose he had a dizzy spell. Them that climb to great heights have a longer way to fall."

Mathilde laughs, veritably cackles, making Mary almost smile.

"Leave me to it, now. Would you?" Mary says.

"No." Mathilde reaches to her seared hair and pulls a clump out, flesh coming with it. As she studies the unstable mass, blood runs down her temple, follows the course of her jaw, and drips from her chin. It disappears into the earth. She drops the clump of hair and picks at the wound on her head, pulling raw pieces out and examining them one by one. "Eager beaver," she chastises, not looking up. "You couldn't wait for nature to take its course?"

"Nature is unpredictable. Not everyone suffers equally, for instance." Mary reaches around Mathilde and cuts the rabbit down.

"We had an expression in Little Germany. *Der Mensch denkt und Gott lenkt.* It means, in case you're wondering: 'Man plans and God laughs.'"

"What of it?"

She drops the last bit of hair, and it disappears into the ground. "Aren't we grumpy today."

"Do not second-guess me."

Mathilde was right about the turn of the Soper tide, but Mary has begun to revise her estimation of the woman's deeper wisdom. You do not get to fry helplessly with your children in a man-made fire and still claim to know more than Mary about survival. Why did she not think of that years ago?

She holds up the rabbit and looks it over, finding the remnant of a lettuce leaf protruding from its teeth. Stupid creature. A premature desire to outrun the coming winter made him impatient and careless. She won't risk the same mistake.

Back inside, she guts the rabbit, cuts off its head, hangs it unskinned upside down from a pipe to let the blood run out. She may never get to eat it, but old habits die hard. Survival, that's the main thing. Everyone underestimates the survivor while crediting chance. Everyone underestimates Mary. Until, that is, they find themselves looking up at her from a pine box.

She kept her head down on North Brother for so many years that people rarely got a good look at her face. She would run into some of the longer-tenured nurses, and they would startle. "Oh, Mary. It's you. You gave me a scare."

"I'm sorry, miss."

The cottage that served as her cell had a small stove. She cooked her own meals there and fed the occasional rat but never another person. For nearly twenty years, she reported to the old Smallpox Hospital to help out, but when big staff turnover came one year, she started showing up less frequently. They had little use for her, anyway, and she turned her attention to taking longer and longer walks around the island, restlessness carrying her along, messages floating to her from the *General Slocum* dead. She could see that no one else perceived the voices, and at first she thought the ghosts would drive her mad. But then she grew accustomed to them. When she stopped fighting to tune them out and began to listen, they helped her even more to understand the fundamental injustices of the world. Expressing jealousy at her physical endurance, they made her grasp how special she was, too. And, most important, they gave her ideas of how to achieve retribution, the thing she lived for.

One day, a patient approximately Mary's age arrived on the island of her own free will. "But my, she looks remarkably like you, Mary," Mr. Cunningham observed as they stood on the dock, Mary checking off names on a clipboard.

"She does indeed, sir."

She would not befriend that woman, of course—she trusted no one. But she kept an eye on Dolores Hannity, who proved to be another Irishwoman from the north. When she got the opportunity, Mary sneaked peeks at her medical records. She was in for tuberculosis, but she had survived polio and typhoid fever, too, the poor wretch. Mary, on the pretense of helping straighten her bedsheets, got close one quiet morning and sniffed. Something special that Mary, with the help of the shaded world, had learned to discern. Not just a survivor of typhoid fever, but a carrier, too!

After that discovery, Mathilde became more assertive. "I brought her here," she claimed one night in the cottage.

"You did not."

"How else to explain the resemblance?"

"One lives long enough, and eventually one's double comes along."

"Almost. Almost a *Doppelgänger*. Not quite." She was practically reading Mary's thoughts. She sat watching her stew a bit, then spoke up again. "How will you overcome the eyes?" No one had Mary's eyes.

Mary scowled. "I'll think of something."

Good things come to those who wait.

Over several years, the hospital staff turned over considerably, and Mary had little contact with them anymore. Those she did see, she tried not to give a good look at her. With the Depression, more laborers piled onto North Brother, too many hands for too little work, and Mary receded further into the background, came closer to being forgotten.

A change of seasons arrived, summer into fall. One night in September, a storm brewed while Mary sat listening to "I'm Getting Sentimental Over You," performed by Tommy Dorsey and His Orchestra. Outside, lightning flashed bright, illuminating the curtains, followed at once by a deep rumble that rattled windows and shook the floorboards under her feet. The radio cut off and the lights went out. In the wind, a loose shutter banged on the west side of the cottage. Mary went to secure it and found Mathilde standing there.

"Dolores Hannity is caught out on a walk, the north path," she said. "Hurry!"

Mary took up her carving fork. She found Dolores alone in the shade of an old tree, disoriented, boxing her own ears. The ghostly voices were strong; she must be hearing them, too. Mary watched as they tormented the woman, driving her to the brink of insanity. Even in fading light, in the rain, under a tree, she could see that her face had turned several shades of purple. A moment later, her mouth contorted and she collapsed to her knees and fell over twitching.

Only then did Mary approach closer. Years ago, the nurses had taught her to read vital signs, and she quickly established that the unconscious Dolores yet lived. Quickly, with great effort tugging at clothing in the rain and wind, she undressed Dolores and undressed herself, momentarily leaving them both naked. The woman moaned and twitched but could not fight her way back to consciousness. Mary finished her task, redressing them both in one another's clothing. She had long ago traded in the bland uniform of a patient for the stripes of an aide, but after a few moments, there she stood looking like a patient again.

Only one detail remained. Mary took out her carving fork, aligned the tines on either side of the bridge of the woman's nose, and pressed the sharp points into the eyeballs. They popped with a revolting wet sound. Dolores, fully comatose by now, did not respond to the pain. Mary took the woman's hands by the wrists like she was working a marionette and plunged the fingertips into her bloody eyes.

Now to finish her. Mary raised her fork to pierce the jugular, but then she hesitated. If she made the woman look like a suicide, she'd have to leave her precious fork behind. If a murder, they'd comb the island looking for a weapon. What course to take? She'd have to leave the fork, she concluded—perhaps a fitting outcome, as she'd also be leaving Mary behind forever. But just as she raised it to strike, a splash of headlights washed through the trees, a pickup truck coming round the bend. Mary tucked the fork into her pocket and ducked into the woods just ahead of the headlights. The truck came to an abrupt stop and she ran.

She ran as fast as possible through the storm and stowed the fork in the secret room that she had furnished for herself behind a hidden door in the garret of the Smallpox Hospital, precisely as she would later replicate this private space when they constructed the Tuberculosis Pavilion.

The hospital staff had just changed over, soaked newcomers stamping their feet and shaking out their umbrellas. Mary-dressed-as-Dolores, dripping wet, appeared in a corner of the hallway. She must have looked an unrecognizable wreck. She averted her face and waved for the attention of the chief physician on duty—a new man, fresh to the island just nine days ago.

"Doctor, come quick," she said in an urgent whisper. "It's Mary Mallon. She's lying out on the path and something terrible has happened. Something terrible indeed!"

Karalee

AT FIRST SHE is simply unwilling to believe. How can the pale face with the bloody eyes belong to Gerard? She drops to a knee and rests a hand on his still stomach. He feels remarkably cold, but only because she expected warmth. In reality, he is probably the temperature of the air, a fact that she grasps as a sliver of hope. She hears herself ask, "Is he breathing?"

Chick's face contorts as if the question appalls him, but then he plucks a hair from his own head and holds it over Gerard's partially open mouth. The hair flutters.

Estela, encouraged by this, lays her right ear on Gerard's sternum and listens for a long few seconds. "No heartbeat. It's just the wind." She shakes her head and sits back up on her knees.

They kneel poised on the breakwater beside him, sharp gray boulders digging into their knees and shins but no one demonstrating the least bit of physical discomfort. Inside is another matter. Inside, Karalee's chest aches. She watches Estela inhale a long, extended breath and let out a wail that goes on forever. Fat tears seep from the corners of her eyes.

Karalee realizes that every one of her friends is red-faced and crying. "How?" she says. "How does this happen?"

She looks around to them for answers, but none are forthcoming.

Their faces have become a blur. Her experience of the world feels even hazier than when she was stoned last night. A milky glaze lies over everything.

Josh removes his spectacles and rubs his eyes. "I can't look at this," he says. "I can't look at this." He replaces his glasses and, with some effort, pulls the bottom of Gerard's T-shirt up over his face, just far enough to cover the empty eye sockets.

Karalee pats the bare chest, runs her hand over the smooth skin. Though cool, it feels so firm and vibrant, so ready to be engaged, so human. How can all prospect of movement have departed?

When she looks up again, they have all separated. Josh paces the beach, rubbing his eyes. Chick stands aside, coursing his fingers through his hair, as if working up the courage to pull it out in clumps. Estela, still on the rocks, has crawled toward the water and lies with her face buried under her bent right arm, as if a big wave just deposited her onto shore.

With a fidgety surge, Karalee stands so abruptly that the barbecue fork, still tucked into the band of her shorts, pokes her in the back between her shoulder blades. She lingers by Gerard, pinching her upper lip between thumb and forefinger.

They mourn this way for a long time, each occupying their own world: sobbing, crying aloud, mindlessly repeating useless gestures, touching themselves as if to affirm their continued presence in the physical world. Finally, they come together again a few feet from Gerard. It occurs to Karalee that she's never before seen a human body in this state, let alone that of a friend. Gerard's stillness amazes her in a way that defies the obvious. "He has found peace," the clerics are fond of saying. But there is no peace here. A stranger, walking up, would know in an instant that Gerard is not sleeping, not merely unconscious, not placid. He is too still. Inanimate. Without life. Why can't she say it to herself?

He is dead.

A gust of wind passes through them, sending a chill across the back of her neck and whistling through the ruins of nearby buildings. The sound brings back to mind the wails of last night. Never before did she believe in ghosts or an afterlife. Now she wonders whether Gerard's soul will join the tumultuous chorus that occupies this horrid island. She recalls him standing by the window, looking out into darkness as the spirits clamored. Did curiosity get the best of him? But even so, why would he end up out here, dead?

The iron tower that they originally took for a kind of lighthouse is not an enclosed structure. Nearby stands what once served as the actual lighthouse, the shell of a Dutch gable building with its roof collapsed and the remains of a tower lying on its side. Whatever constituted the beacon on top has long been destroyed or disassembled, no visible remains of the lenses. The structure beneath which Gerard lies is the less substantial steel latticework tower, originally painted white, although now it shows rust and huge swaths of peeling paint. At the top sits a battered foghorn mechanism with a pipe rail running around it.

Chick stares up at the foghorn with his hands on his hips. "You can see there that the railing is bent and broken. Gerard climbed up to the top, leaned against the rail, and fell. He was always clumsy."

"That doesn't explain what the hell he was doing up there," Josh says, his brow knitted in anger.

"Well, what's up there? The horn—he may have been trying to fix the foghorn."

"The horn works on electricity, and there is none here. Do you think he didn't know that?"

"Maybe he went up for the view."

"In the dark of night?"

"There are lighted things to see at all hours." Chick pauses, churns a hand through thin air. "Work with me here. I'm just testing out theories."

"Test out this theory," Josh snaps. "Arrogant rule-breaking professor endangers life of his students through irresponsible boating practices."

Chick bridles. "Whoa. Down, boy."

"You mean 'Down, Jewboy'?"

Chick rolls his eyes. "We're all adults here, right? I'm not in loco parentis. Besides which, coming to this island wasn't my idea."

"I told you not to."

"We decided as a group. Gerard wanted to come, remember."

"It's a damn high price to pay."

"Granted." Chick sighs. "Do you have something substantive to contribute to the discussion of Gerard's situation? Or do you intend to persist with this negativity?"

"We're not in class anymore, Chick. Gerard's not in a situation. He's dead. He didn't go up that tower to find something or to do something. How about that for a theory? He went up there to escape something."

"What could he possibly be escaping?"

Josh removes his glasses again and rubs his eyes so hard that Karalee fears he will injure himself. "I don't know. We were all so wasted. Maybe he had a bad trip. He's done LSD in the past. Maybe the ludes gave him a flashback. Maybe he was sleepwalking."

"He was following the voices," Karalee says in a monotone. "He climbed over or somehow avoided the cot that was blocking the doorway in the ward. In the middle of the night, I saw him standing at the window."

"You did?" Estela says. "Oh, honey. Why didn't you stop him?"

"I had no idea what he planned to do." Tears roll down her face, tickle her cheeks. She wipes them away with a knuckle. "That was the last I saw of him alive."

Josh slides his glasses back on. "This is crazy. We can only save ourselves, can't change what happened to Gerard. His accident is a matter for the police, for the coroner. We need to get rescued." He surveys the breakwater, identifies the tallest spot within sight, and works his way over there, hopping from one boulder to another. For all his effort, Karalee observes, he has gained no more than two vertical feet. It's absurd. But when he gets there, he begins waving his arms and calling across the river for help. After a few minutes, he turns to the others and urges, "C'mon, you guys."

They all join in. The Sewer Rats. Trapped. Waving her arms, Karalee shrieks, "Help! Over here! Help!" But another word keeps drifting up to the forefront of her mind: *cage cage cage.* She pushes it away, screams louder, and gesticulates with increased urgency. There are many boats out on the river, but they are too far away for her to make out the people on them. Which means no one can see her or Estela or Chick or Josh, no matter how desperately they wave their arms. No one can hear them, no matter how loudly they call. From a distance, they may as well be veins of quartz in the rocks they stand upon. Bright up close. Invisible from afar.

Despite this fact, they continue their efforts. After an hour of near-constant bellowing, they have finally exhausted themselves to such a degree that they collapse, one by one, onto their butts on the boulders beneath them. There is silence but for the occasional call of a seagull, the scouring rush of the river, the whining engines of airplanes and helicopters moving through the sky way beyond their reach. And Karalee's thoughts run to her father.

The *Flagellum* brought them here. Chick brought them here—commanding the tiller. She brought them here—pointing at a map. But most of all, her father brought them here. *Soper Soap Cleans Cleanest!* With stubborn persistence, he brought Karalee here as surely as George A. Soper brought Mary Mallon.

She reaches for the scar on her left ear and scratches it. She closes her eyes and her head lolls, all she can do to keep herself from fainting into a crevasse and wedging between the boulders. She is so tired. Let the chasm come up and swallow her. But then what would the point have been? Instead, she will live through this. She will bring back to her father the pictures of this ruined paradise upon which his family's reputation is constructed. Then she'll announce that she's leaving public health and Havermeyer University behind in order to pursue her real passion.

A passion is something you can't help doing, like she can't keep her hands off her camera. Maybe her father's true passion is bossing people around, and soap is merely his instrument. Maybe Mary Mallon's passion was cooking, and all the misery she brought upon others and herself was just a consequence of her inability to stop doing what she loved. Without the ability to pursue that passion, she may as well have disappeared.

Did she disappear? No. Isolation is not disappearance.

Chick's voice rises behind Karalee. Urging them to go. They can't sit here forever, chins on their chests. One by one, they work their way back to the base of the steel tower.

"Don't we need to bury Gerard?" Estela asks, flinching from a glance at the body.

"This isn't one of those Western movies, where we bang together a rudimentary cross," Chick says. "When we get help . . . he gets help."

"He's beyond help," Josh intones.

"Gets a dignified burial, back home on the mainland. That's what I meant."

"I agree with you there. There's nothing dignified about this place."

"There never was," says Karalee. "That's why they made the buildings so grand. They were lying to themselves. To everyone. It was a big lie."

Chick recoils. "Listen to you, the queen of overstatement. Make that your Ph.D. thesis, why dontcha? Meanwhile, there's one living person who knows this island best. We need to press Mary to come up with a solution for us."

"Mary Mallon?" asks Estela.

"Let's stop with the Typhoid Mary nonsense. The woman who calls herself Mary—the homeless woman. She must have a plan for getting out of here when the food runs out."

"She has plans for the future?" Estela wonders, then sighs. "I guess it's a possibility, anyway."

In unison they direct their gaze out to the churning river. An appreciable storm must have passed to the north, because the water has grown more turgid in the time they've been out here. Karalee watches floating trash and large limbs of trees whisking by, a testament to its profound force. The trees drag fingers of organic material behind them. They remind her of the kinked fibers of witches' brooms.

WITH THE ONSET of afternoon, clouds have invaded the bright morning sky. The low overcast magnifies Karalee's growing sense of confinement.

In the plaza, strung out with anxiety, they argue about whether to go inside looking for the homeless woman, whom Josh has begun referring to as "the slattern." He plays endlessly with his glasses, as if he can't find a comfortable place for them to rest on his face any longer.

"It's rat infested," Josh says of the Tuberculosis Pavilion. "The slattern is feeding them with her filthy habits."

"Rats are unavoidable," Karalee says. "Even with modern health codes, New York can't get rid of them. What hope does Mary have?"

"She might fight back against the filth—at least in one or two corners of this godforsaken place. She's had plenty of time to do so, by the looks of things."

"You know what I think?" says Chick. "I think this is just the way she likes it. Her presence here is an act of protest against the whole notion of cleanliness. Strikingly like Typhoid Mary herself, when you think about it. That's one reason she chooses to stay here."

"Which doesn't mean we shouldn't go inside," Estela says. "She may be the one person who can help us."

Josh's face has gone pale. He bites his fingernails.

Chick looks him over with contempt. "I'll go find the woman myself, if that's what it takes."

"What a hero you've proved to be, Professor," Josh says.

Chick ignores him. "She won't be hard to find. We know all her haunts by now. You all can wait out here, if you want."

"I'll go with Chick," Karalee volunteers.

"No." Estela straightens her shoulders. "We're in this together. Sewer Rats, right? You can do this, Josh." She takes his hand and tugs.

"Yeah," Chick says. "The woman will protect you."

"I didn't say I needed protection," Josh snaps. "It's disgusting, that's all. We spent the night inside for shelter because we had to. We dealt with it. But Gerard had the right idea. Our salvation is out here, not in there."

"And how'd that work out for Gerard?"

"I don't know. He escaped, didn't he?"

"Now you're talking nonsense."

With Estela still grasping his hand, Josh follows them inside. They don't find the homeless woman in her kitchen, but they see signs of her presence. In particular, the dead rabbit hanging headless. On the floor beneath it, a thousand green bottle flies, bubbling in a lumpy mass, wage frantic battle over a puddle of blood.

Josh twists his face in disgust, his lower lip trembling. He seizes their old cooler, which still lies open on the floor, lifts it over his head and smashes the bottom down on the flies with a clatter. The insects scatter with an angry chaotic buzzing, and Josh madly swings his arms around, fending them off. Finally, after he exhausts himself, he stands in place, staring blankly, a saturnine zombie.

"Feel better?" Estela says, losing patience with him.

"Bedlam." He casts his gaze around. "This is what happens when civilization departs. I don't see how a madwoman is going to lead us from here to the promised land." He sniffles, crinkles his face.

"Look," Karalee says. "Your nose is bleeding."

"Great." Josh reaches up and feels it. He glances down at the blood on his fingers, wipes the tip of his nose with his shirt. Another bead of blood forms, drips to the floor.

"It's not that bad," Karalee says. "Has this ever happened to you before?"

"Once or twice as a kid, I guess."

Chick sighs. "A consultation with the homeless woman, that's all I'm calling for. She's been around long enough to work every angle. Maybe she knows where there's a telephone, for instance."

Karalee bites a lip, thinking. She may have spotted a battered phone or two attached to a wall or lying in a pile of rubbish. It doesn't seem likely that any such thing might still function, but anything's worth a try.

They depart the pavilion and soon enough find Mary in the boiler house, sitting by a small fire. Karalee has the sense they interrupted her in midsentence, though of course no one was present before they walked in.

"We found our friend," Estela says. "He's d—" She chokes and sobs, suddenly overcome. "Fell from the lighthouse or whatever that thing is. We need to get help."

"No doubt," Mary says, staring off.

"Is there a functioning telephone around or some other way to signal the mainland?"

The woman twists her jaw, works at a tooth with her tongue. "Only way I can think is wait for another vandal to come. Hitch a ride."

"We're not waiting," Josh says, bouncing on the balls of his feet. He turns to Chick. "I say we swim for it. The water's still warm enough, end of summer. The Bronx shore's only three or four hundred yards away."

"Ay." Mary sees him wipe at his nose and look at the blood on his index finger. "But stronger men have tried. None ever made it. The current runs against you here. In the other direction, you're well into Hell Gate. Of course, no matter which way you set out, you'll end up in Hell Gate anyway. For a swimmer? Well, that river may as well be an ocean with a constant riptide. If you want to get to the other side alive, it's impassable without a craft."

Karalee recalls the most recent look she had at the swirling brown water. Filled with heavy flotsam, it seemed more unforgiving than ever. "She's right," she says. "Swimming is out of the question."

"We have to try something." Josh pinches the bridge of his nose.

"Drown if you want," says Mary. "Makes no difference to me. The world sure don't need another sanitation engineer."

A thought crosses Chick's mind. "If we sit tight two more days, they'll notice us missing in class Monday. At that point, someone at Havermeyer will figure out that the *Fledge* is gone, and the Coast Guard will undertake a search. They'll trace our steps and find us eventually."

"No. No." Josh shakes his head vehemently. "That leaves too much to chance." He looks into the furnace. On the floor beside it lie a few logs of split wood. He peels off a thick splinter, lights it in the fire, and holds it aloft with the tip aflame. "A fire brought us here and a fire can rescue us. We'll light the place up and they'll come running."

"You won't!" Mary jumps up, grabs the splinter from him, throws it to the ground, and stamps it out with her bare foot.

The outburst so startles Karalee that her hand goes to her chest. It is the first time they have seen the homeless woman flash anger.

"Think of the *General Slocum*," Mary growls. "A fire might consume this whole island before anyone gets rescued. And what makes you think the authorities won't just let it burn to the ground on purpose? My home."

"Your rat-infested pigsty," Josh says.

"Josh!" Estela cries. "Don't be rude!"

Disappointment and betrayal cross his face. He searches Estela's eyes, unbelieving, pained. His gaze shifts to his other two friends. Chick's nostrils flare. Karalee feels her sympathy fall in the woman's direction, not with Josh. They are the intruders here, after all, invading Mary's space. Bad luck may have befallen them, but they brought it on themselves. They have no right to sacrifice Mary's interests in service to their own.

Josh, seeing he has no allies, throws up his hands. "Have it your way." He storms from the building with extended strides. A crash echoes from behind the boilers—a door slamming or some hard object thrown down.

A long silence follows.

"I apologize for my friend," Estela says. "His nerves are frayed."

"He might show some respect," Mary says. "People have rights."

Chick runs a hand through his ponytail and adjusts the hair tie. "We'll wait for the Coast Guard," he repeats. "That's the plan. Might take a couple of days, but our options are nil. It's safer than sky-high flames or a swim across the channel by a long shot."

Mary nods, satisfied they won't be burning her island to cinders. "If you're staying," she concedes, "I'll cook dinner again. May as well. 'When a man's stomach is full, it makes no difference whether he's rich or poor.' Did you like last night's bread?"

Karalee can't imagine eating, visions still swimming through her brain of Gerard's hollowed-out eyes.

"Very much." Estela answers so quickly that it could only be motivated by politeness.

"Good, then," replies Mary. "I'll bake some fresh. Plus a surprise or two."

Mary

DOUGH DOESN'T KNEAD itself, she has always been fond of saying. She already has a risen mound set aside in a cool place. She stands at the counter working it with her hands, thinking how much she missed cooking back then, once she had set in motion her scheme to disappear.

Mary-who-was-Dolores lay in a coma in the Smallpox Hospital for six years while Dolores-who-was-Mary made herself scarce. When she finally found the bed empty one early morning, the real Mary heaved a sigh of relief.

In the person of Dolores, she requested to attend the interment of ashes at Saint Raymond's Cemetery in the Bronx. As a priest intoned the Our Father, she stood beside two fellow patients and three staff nurses, all of whom expressed pity without knowing that the subject of their sympathy stood beside them. The headstone read toward the top: MARY MALLON DIED NOV 11, 1938. And toward the bottom: JESUS MERCY.

As they walked in silence to the car that would take them back to the North Brother ferry, one of the nurses remarked, "I wonder if, in the end, she understood that it didn't have to be this way."

Mary bit her tongue so hard, she nearly cried out in pain. With her false sympathy, what did this nurse—or any of them—know about the lack of freedom under which Mary and the other quarantined patients operated? The nurse went home every weekend to her family and would continue to do so while Mary rotted in her hell—never even saw Briehof again, as Mathilde so often reminds her.

Walking through the cemetery in the company of these unsuspecting women and the unknowing priest, she began to reconsider her plan of escape, which initially had her excusing herself for the ladies' room, then running for her life, straight out the cemetery gate, disappearing into the neighborhood of Throggs Neck. But doing so, she suddenly saw, would only cause her true identity to be revealed. Before the cremation, she heard, doctors had performed an autopsy on the body they thought was Mary Mallon. They found live typhoid bacteria in her gallbladder, which sealed the case against not only Mary but also every healthy carrier like her. Even if they didn't sniff out the change of identity, if they thought that Dolores—a known carrier—had run, they would track her down like a dog. In any case, Dolores-who-was-Mary had no good plan yet to counter the power of the state, despite years of seething over its abuse of her.

Therefore, for some time still, she had to be content with having finally shimmied out from under her particular mark of Cain. In the public imagination, Typhoid Mary now lay forever in the grave. What no one could imagine: Mary Mallon secretly lived.

More than that. In her way, she thrived. For as she had watched Dolores waste away in that hospital bed, Mary changed, but not as expected. She put on heft, but gained strength. She lost touch with those around her, but her senses grew in acuity. She receded from one part of the world, but made contact with aspects of existence that most people never see.

She no longer aged physically, in other words. Rather, she evolved.

With access to her cottage gone and no need to publicly enter the wards, Mary pursued her own ideal of hygiene. Which was to say, very little at all. Around the time that Soper died—in 1948, the doctors whispered of it and she saw the obituary with her own eyes—Mary's transformation had almost become complete. She had well settled in her secret room in the new Tuberculosis Pavilion and discovered that every step she took away from humanity was a step in the direction of her own way of being. She had been selfish before, the great man said. But now, for the first time, Mary truly embraced selfishness, because she had only herself to please.

Ring around the rosie.

She has some pumpkins from the garden that she can make into a soup. As she works, she recalls the cemetery where her gravestone stands. Congested but pastoral, much like North Brother looked when she first arrived. Now the trees and parasitic vines crowd out everything. She tires of beating them back. She does not know how just yet, but the Soper girl must be the mechanism of her release.

The young man Josh had a nosebleed, meaning that the typhoid from her hand is taking hold much quicker than expected. All those years simmering in its own juices—in her juices—have made it potent. And that boy Josh is a disrespectful know-it-all. In her experience, her disease always claims the most impertinent first. She will soon say good riddance to that one.

Mathilde, appearing, sings a nursery rhyme in German to the tune of "Ring Around the Rosie."

Mary has the taste of copper in her mouth. "You again." She frowns.

"Hush, hush, hush. You can't get rid of me. I'm in you."

"What are you saying with your foreign rhymes?"

"You'll have that whole gang on their knees before long, that's what."

"Lower than their knees," Mary snarls. She waves her carving fork. The flies depart along with Mathilde.

All fall down.

Soper and his associates saw Mary as no threat to their privileges, so long as they kept her bottled up. But they did not think, because they could not conceive, what would happen when the stopper came off that bottle.

She bided her time all those long years, withdrawing farther and farther into the background, like the typhoid bacilli that hide in the folds of her organs. As the island passed through its mortal permutations, she traversed it like a wraith, hiding in her secret room, stealing from the pantry late at night, meditating on her revenge. As she meditates upon it to this day.

So long it has been. Yet so fresh burns her anger.

The young man Gerard felt it. Already disoriented by the ghost voices—as guileful as sirens, tempting him—he had little sense of where to run when she jumped out at him with her carving fork in the night. But, wanting it to appear as an accident, she knew exactly where to drive him. Up he went. Up. Climbing like a dizzy monkey, losing his flip-flops, the rusted steel slicing into his feet. In the moonlight, she thought she saw satisfaction settle in his dark eyes. Surely, he must have concluded, the ungainly woman could not touch him up here. Another who underestimated her at his own peril. She mounted the tower and followed with her usual relentlessness.

As it turned out, she did not have to lay a finger on him. When she was one rung away, he leaned hard on the railing and it gave way, careless man. The beginning of disease may have corrupted his reflexes, but no doubt Mathilde will take credit. In any case, he landed upon the rocks with a crack, barely heard by Mary over the racket that the spirits raised all around her. He was no Captain Van Schaick, but as a long-awaited sacrifice, he served his purpose. Their voices rose up with joy.

She climbed down and waited on the rocks to see what they would do. For a long hour, it was only more sounds, their wails circling in a vortex. When that faded, the seagull came as if summoned from a far-off place. She watched for a while as it plucked at the open eyes, as if yanking meat from the inside of a clam—bringing back to her thoughts of Dolores.

Mary grins at the memory as she kneads her dough. Those eyes. Blind to her power in life. Blind in death. Yet a man can still be destroyed by that which he cannot see.

Karalee

WHERE DID THE afternoon go? Under darkening clouds, daytime already hangs on the cusp of evening. Estela's dusky skin has assumed an olive hue. Her energy ebbs low, and she carries her bad arm as a heavy burden. When Karalee asks whether she's feeling well, she shakes off the inquiry with a flash of pride. While there's still light, Karalee snaps her portrait, planning to use it for comparison someday. A document of this sad little adventure.

They leave the boiler house on a mission to find a working telephone. It's a long shot, everyone agrees, but the realities of Chick's plan to await the Coast Guard have begun to weigh on them. As daylight fades, the prospect of spending another night on North Brother takes on a different aspect, especially with Gerard lying dead on the other end of the island. Suddenly, her mind flashes on the seagull pecking at her friend. She shudders to think what will happen if the rats find his body. But a thread of annoyance creeps in, the tiny thought arising that it serves him right for wandering off and putting them all in this position. She closes her eyes, shakes her head, and rubs her face as if to abrade the callousness away.

At the old ward where they slept last night, they find the cots all back in a row, mattresses in their places. A small sleeve of Nilla wafers rests on each pillow. Karalee runs a hand across the back of her clammy neck, thinking again of Gerard.

"The woman likes to feed people," Chick says, picking up one of the packages and examining it. "But I'm not stoned anymore." He drops it to the floor and crushes it underfoot.

"Will we sleep here tonight?" Estela asks.

"Where else?" says Karalee.

They comb the Tuberculosis Pavilion, finding three telephones: two without cords, lying in piles of rubble, and a third attached to the wall. Estela jumps at that one and puts the receiver to her ear. She repeatedly presses the switch hook but eventually concedes that it's dead. When she drops the handset, Karalee watches hypnotized as it twirls at the end of the cord, batting against the wall.

She says, "You'd think Josh would've come back and found us by now."

"Why would he?" says Chick. "He's wrapped up in his own shit."

"He was just disappointed," Estela says. "It's been a hard day for all of us."

"Yeah, but he was the one raving like a lunatic. Maybe—" Chick catches himself.

Karalee thinks she knows what he started to say. That Josh hit the river and swam for it. Another thought she wants to perish. She keeps having them.

"My voice is hoarse. I'm not shouting all over this island for him," Chick says, exasperated. "But when he turns up again, we'll welcome him like a brother. Deal?"

"Stop telling us what to do," Karalee says.

They abandon the pavilion and pick their way through several more buildings, finding no more telephones, working or otherwise. Everything is beginning to feel eerily familiar. In the gymnasium, they collapse on the floor just where they sat yesterday morning, although that feels to Karalee like a lifetime ago.

Estela rests her head against the wall, staring up at the damaged ceiling. Chick drums his fingers on a weathered floorboard, muttering, "There has to be an angle that we're missing here."

"You remind me of my father," Karalee says. "He's always convinced that there's a hidden entrance to the cave full of treasure, just feet away from wherever he's standing, if only he could find it."

Chick lifts an eyebrow.

"Why's the treasure always in a cave in these stories, anyway?" Estela wonders.

"That's where the dragon guards it."

"But man invented dragons. They're not real."

"He invented the treasure in the cave, too. In my dad's case, it's a cave full of soap. Soper Soap Cleans Cleanest! Did I ever tell you that slogan, Chick?" No answer. "Chick?"

Chick, on hands and knees, has crawled to the nearby heating grate. He's squinting through the iron latticework. "I think I see something."

"A phone down there?" Estela asks groggily.

"No. Give me a hand with this grate, Kiki. Would you?"

She stares at him.

"Please?"

The grate is heavy and sticky, but it was meant to come out. After several strong heaves, it yields. Chick flips it aside with a crash. Karalee, who has given up all efforts to keep clean, wipes her hands on her shorts. "It's a heating line."

"We knew that already," Estela says.

Chick points in past the edge of the hole, to the floor of the large metal duct. "There's a footprint there. A bare footprint."

"You think Gerard?" Estela says. "He was barefoot when we found him."

"No." Chick shakes his head. "The woman."

He sits on the edge of the hole and lowers himself down. When his heels hit, the sound echoes through the shaft. "This goes on awhile," he says, crouching down and peering. "Like catacombs. I can't see, though. Too dark." He ponders for a moment. "Let me borrow your flash, Kiki."

Reluctantly, she parts with her camera. Chick points it and fires off the flash, peers in and blinks a few times. "Yep. I'm going spelunking."

"Not without us, you aren't," Estela says, her enthusiasm for adventure rebounding—or is it her reluctance to let anyone else peel away from them? With Karalee's help, she lowers her body into the duct. Chick extends a hand, but Karalee jumps in by herself.

The shaft is about four feet high, so they can proceed on foot, but only while awkwardly bent over. Every fifteen feet or so, Chick fires the flash. Though it blinds them for a fraction of a second, an image imprints on their memory long enough to discern the way forward. They feel their way along in the dark until the uncertainty begins inducing panic; then Chick fires the flash again.

They go along about a hundred feet in this manner until Chick presses the button and nothing happens. The flash has died. "Aw, shit. That was bound to happen," he says, passing the camera back.

It's warm and stuffy in the tunnel. Humid. Chick and Estela's pungent body odor slaps Karalee in the face, and she knows she must smell just as bad to them. Riding the odor, a fearful sense of déjà vu grips her, carrying her mind back to her dream of the crate—it's a dog-crate cage, that's what it is!—accompanied now by a large helping of claustrophobia.

"Why are we doing this?"

"She came this way, that's why," Chick answers. "I don't trust her. Maybe it leads to something she doesn't want us to see." He pauses. "Wait, shouldn't there be loads of spiderwebs in here? There are no spiderwebs."

"She fed us," says Karalee.

"She had her reasons."

They walk a few steps and a few more and a few more, feeling their way along, the sheet metal yielding to more solid cast iron. The walls are cool and smooth under Karalee's fingertips, then occasionally sharp at a seam. If they'd thought to count the seams, they'd know exactly how far they've gone.

"How much farther, you think?" Karalee asks no one in particular.

Estela says, "Isn't this just going to take us to the boiler house?"

"Maybe," Chick says.

There is a dim shaft of light up ahead now, but not enough to brighten the tunnel. They proceed with caution, still groping along the curved walls, Karalee's back beginning to ache from bending, the handle of the barbecue fork pressing against the base of her spine like a pebble in a shoe. She considers throwing it away, but decides not to. To embrace suffering is to retain options. To give in to suffering is to abandon hope.

The light disappears for a second, but it's only Chick blocking it. They hear a crashing sound as he proceeds, branches snapping. "Bushes!" Chick growls as they emerge outside.

After some examination, they see that the shaft collapsed under the invasion of tree roots. Someone cleared this entrance, hidden behind a large euonymus bush—"burning bush" Estela says—but the rest remains buried. "It's like a bunker. How many more of these?" Chick asks, not expecting a reply. He runs his fingers through his hair and adjusts his ponytail. "She owns this island. Moving in and out of view. Dropping goodies on our pillows. She's fucking with us."

"Why would she?" Karalee says with little conviction.

"I don't know," Chick admits, "but we can't stay." A thought crosses his face. He scratches the stubble on his cheek. "The boathouse. Of course! That's our way out. Remember? One of those boats still floats."

For the first time in hours, Estela's smile revives. "Maybe we'll find Josh there," she says.

SOME SPRING HAS returned to Chick's steps, but Karalee notices that Estela is badly dragging her lame foot. She finds herself wishing they'd taken the Nilla wafers from the ward with them. They could use the sugar.

The side door of the boathouse is jammed open by debris. The building was handsome once, red brick trimmed with rough-cut granite blocks, but the roof has partially caved in. They tramp through piled leaves up to their shins, unseen sticks snapping underfoot. The dock originally ran around three sides of the interior, but the fallen beam buried half of it underwater, so it now drops off like a ramp. Also under the beam lie the remnants of one motorboat, sunk up to its gunwales. The other boat, however, appears to remain seaworthy, floating high in the water. A fiberglass SlickCraft with an outboard motor and a cherry red padded interior, it's not so different from Chick's boat. It is filthy, though, like everything here. Mildew covers the cushions, which have largely been shredded by rodents, fat tufts of yellowish foam poking through—like pictures Karalee has seen of human belly fat protruding from deep incisions.

"That boat's seen better days," Chick says. "But it floats. That's the important thing."

On one side of the boathouse—although reaching it would necessitate wading down the ramp and through the water—hangs an old canoe with the bottom rotted out and, more important, a pair of wooden oars that appear still to be in pretty good shape.

"We can use those," Chick says. "All we have to do is get the door open."

He jumps onto the SlickCraft, steps over the windshield, and crouches on the bow, testing the overhead-style boathouse door with both hands. It won't budge. Not an inch. He looks around. "It's off its tracks. See?"

"Maybe we can use one of the oars," Estela suggests.

Chick, energized, leaves the boat and crashes down the ramp through the water, scrambling back up to the remains of the dock on the other side. The water is only two and a half feet deep. He grabs one oar and splashes his way back across.

But he can't make any headway with the door, the bottom edge of which hangs one tantalizingly small foot above the level of the river. He first tries shoving the guide wheels back into their tracks with the blade of the oar, then attempts to lever up the door from its handle, but nothing budges. It's all frozen. As he continues to meet resistance, he applies more force, Estela urging him on. Finally, he takes a swing at the door in frustration, the oar issuing a sharp crack, like a bat meeting a baseball. With that sound, it's as if something also snaps inside him. He begins beating at everything in sight—the boat hull and the docks, then smashing at the aluminum guide rails and, when that accomplishes nothing, standing on the bow of the boat again and battering at the solid wooden door.

"It's the only goddamn thing in this whole place that's not rotten!" he shouts in the midst of a string of curses. "The only goddamn thing!"

He smashes at it with increasing violence, gasping with exertion, swinging the oar like a mace until it shatters into splinters in his hands and he drops it in disgust.

To Karalee's astonishment, when Chick goes to step onto the dock, he trips and falls to his knees, still sucking wind. The heavy breathing seems to tickle his lungs, and he begins to cough and loses control of himself, reduced to wheezing and hacking, then gagging, until he folds over and pukes into the water, ribbons of drool running down his chin.

Karalee can't find within herself any sympathy after this excessive deployment of testosterone, but Estela goes and rests a hand on Chick's sweaty back. "Are you all right?"

"I'm just dandy." He frowns and forces himself to swallow. "Chick is just dandy." Then he doubles over and dry heaves, his nose an inch from the vomit that now greases the surface of the water.

By the time Chick recovers, a soft rain hisses on dead leaves and it is half dark. As they trudge through the woods, he breaks down and begins calling for Josh, but no answer comes.

"He's not out here," Karalee says, knowing she ought to worry about what happened to Josh. Instead she's thinking what an asshole he turned out to be. Maybe he deserves whatever he gets, as payment for bailing out right at everyone's moment of greatest need.

"He probably went inside somewhere to stay dry," says Estela hopefully.

"I could've used his help with that boathouse door." Chick attempts to kick a branch out of his path, but the branch won't cooperate. He snatches it up in anger and hurls it aside.

Estela says, "With nothing but a wooden paddle, you and Josh and Gerard together couldn't have beaten down that door." Hearing herself associate the still-living Josh—and he is still living; he has to be—with the unfortunate Gerard, her eyes go wide and she covers her open mouth.

"Stop it," Karalee says, taking her by the shoulders and gently shaking her. She needs Estela now. "Just stop it. Josh is fine. Josh isn't climbing any towers."

They arrive back at the pavilion wet and defeated, intending by mere inertia to permit Mary to feed them again, but she's still working on dinner. Another rabbit stew—this one more stew than rabbit. Also pumpkin soup, giving off pungent steam. She acknowledges them with no more than a nod, taking in their bedraggled condition.

"I'll be back," she finally says. "See those pots don't boil over."

In the darkness of the kitchen, the flame of the stove provides the only light. Out the windows, rain and clouds occlude everything, effectively casting a giant shadow over the already dim room.

Karalee, wide-eyed, examines the homeless woman's preparations. A crank-operated mixer rests beside a metal bowl. There are cans of dehydrated milk—for whipped cream?—and cans of peaches. The battered metal pitcher from last night has something syrupy inside. Karalee gives it a sniff. Raspberry sauce, but it looks like viscous blood in the darkness.

At the thought of more peach melba on the menu, or some variation of that, her mouth goes dry. Next to her, Estela waves away the steam from the stewing pot. "I can't eat that again. I can't eat anything again. I don't feel so well."

"What's wrong?"

"I'm nauseous, I'm tired, my head hurts. I just want to lie down."

She rubs her nose and comes away with something dark on her fingertips. When she holds it toward the light of the flame, Karalee sees that it's a red smear of blood.

Mary

If Mary has one regret in life, it revolves around her failure to kill Soper when she had the chance. She might have impaled him with her carving fork when they first met. She might have set Briehof's dog upon him. She might have strangled him with her strong hands for that brief moment when they were alone in the hospital room.

He got his stool sample eventually. They locked her off from the toilet and left her with nothing but a chamber pot. What could she do? She considered a hunger strike, but decided she needed her strength for whatever would come. Self-punishment had never been her style.

She places her dough on the cooking sheet and closes the oven door, thinking the gas has to run out soon. Nothing lasts forever—nothing but Mary. North Brother has outlived its usefulness. She will not face another winter here.

The intruders await her, but she will meet them again only when she is good and ready. The Sewer Rats, she heard them call themselves. Using her tunnels, she has monitored them with great care. Not every second, but more than they would suspect. They grow sick and weak. All, that is, but the Soper girl, who possesses depths of resolve that may escape her own awareness. Mary saw something else in her, a sympathetic eye that she has witnessed too rarely in this tormented life. The Soper girl knows persecution in her own way.

For her whole life, Mary has been tested by constraints. When she was a child in Ireland, they bolted her into the outhouse when she refused to wash properly. Her mother closed her up in the kitchen when she caught her picking her nose. On the boat, authorities locked Mary and her stinking cohort into the bottom deck with the heat and the lurching and the screeching of machinery. In the squalid tenement on Third Avenue, she felt not for a moment free from struggle. When any sense of well-being promised to settle upon her, the sound of the elevated train would shake her to her bones or Briehof would barge in stumbling drunk, breaking things. At work she huddled in her garret rooms while the wails of mourners grated at her. She never dared contemplate how much worse things could be in this life, and then along comes Soper to make things worse indeed.

The aroma of baking dough fills the vast room in which she stands barefoot. She closes her eyes and swoons under its spell. The routines of preparation and cooking have always induced in her a kind of trance, the only time she ever feels close to free. She gave up cooking briefly to escape the oppression, but she would never give it up forever—and certainly not at the command of another. Not for Soper with his claims of social good, not for some judge in his fine black robes, not for prideful Dr. Baker. Not for anyone ever.

Ever is a long time, she acknowledges, touching the oven door.

Ashes to ashes.

With only a few preparations remaining, she goes to the floor grate and lifts it off in one motion. In a moment, she has disappeared into the old heating tunnel.

Karalee

ONE OF THE pots boils over, brown foam flowing forth like volcanic spume and crackling when it hits the flame below. Karalee runs to it and turns down the gas. The kitchen smells of burning food.

Chick and Estela each sprawl out on the dust-coated floor, lethargic. "Where is the woman?" Chick moans. "She's disappeared again."

"I thought you weren't hungry," Karalee says.

"I'm not, but she owes us an accounting. She poisoned us, made us sick."

"Oh, you only exhausted yourself with that outburst in the boat-house."

"And Estela?"

"Maybe she caught a bug. If the woman poisoned us, how come I'm not sick?"

"I wish I knew."

He struggles to his feet in the darkness, Karalee feeling him more than she sees him, and lunges forward and twists all the stove burners to a high flame for light. Now Karalee sees the strands of hair plastered to his forehead by sweat, the stubble on his chin grown scruffy and oily. He rakes his gaze over the cans arrayed on the stainless steel counter. "The ingredients for peach melba—or close enough. You know whose weapon that was."

It did in fact dawn on her minutes ago, and she just as quickly drove it from her mind. "That happened a long time ago," she says dismissively. "A very long time ago."

"Soper identified it as the vector. Although in those days, she used fresh peaches, and I gather these are canned." His jaw drops. His gaze darts around the room. "My God. That woman who's been feeding us really is the killer Typhoid Mary."

"That's impossible and you know it," Karalee protests.

His eyes widen. "She's Typhoid Mary and you're defending her."

"Doubly impossible."

"Impossible, yet everything points to it. The name—she told us herself she was Mary. Her slipup with the mention of Briehof. Her cooking skills—everyone always admitted that Mary could cook. And this is North Brother, after all, where she was last seen alive."

"Correction," Karalee says. "Where she was last seen dead."

"Well, I can't explain it, but the rest fits. Don't you agree, Estela?"

Estela looks half asleep, but she's been tracking the conversation. "It's suspicious," she says. "But she's the wrong age."

"How do you know? She's filthy," Chick presses. "We can never get a good look at her face."

"She's not a hundred and thirteen under that grime," Karalee scoffs. Her mind turns over the possibilities. "She could be an imitator," she admits.

"I have another theory," Chick says, warming to his argument. "There's no evidence Mary—the original Mary—ever suffered from typhoid fever, and yet she carried the live bacteria. She was resistant . . . immune. That woman—you saw her. She's a fucking bull. Whatever makes her immune to typhoid could make her immune to other things, maybe even to the accumulated insults of aging. She's Super Woman, but she's not one of the good guys. She's a virago."

"A what?" Estela asks.

"A violent woman with a mean streak. You get my drift? And she's targeted us because . . . because—" He holds up a finger, hitting upon it. "—because of who you are, Karalee. Because of what your great-grandfather did to her."

Karalee swallows hard. "Then why aren't I sick?"

"I—I don't know. Not everyone gets it."

"The incubation period," says Karalee, "is normally weeks."

"Normally," Chick admits, "but there's nothing normal here. Maybe she's got hold of a superbug. Maybe it built and built inside her to a point of extraordinary virulence."

"If she made us sick," says Estela, "can she make us better?"

"Only antibiotics can make us better—presuming this isn't an antibiotic-resistant mutation. I read a paper that said antibiotic overuse is breeding these resistant bacteria that will one day overwhelm all our advances. People blithely consume this stuff, and they're inadvertently breeding stronger and stronger strains. The overuse, in other words, far from helping people, is a long-term hazard to the public health." He harrumphs. "Oh, isn't this rich? Antibiotics are everywhere except for here on this abandoned island, where we most need them."

"You don't know there aren't any here," Estela says. "Maybe she has a secret stash."

Chick likes that idea. "Yes, maybe." He turns back to Karalee. "Did she slip you a few antibiotics yesterday when no one was looking? Huh, Kiki? Could it be that's why you're standing there in the pink while Estela and I—" He coughs and dry heaves. "Estela and I—"

"Are you accusing me of betraying you, Chick?" The thought truly appalls her. "I'd do anything to get you off this island."

"That so? Dead or alive?" He puts his nose in the air and sniffs. "Smell that, Estela?"

"The burning?"

"No. Above that. Something sweeter."

"Hmm. I guess so. Bread baking."

"Yes."

"She's cooking somewhere. Where is she, Kiki?"

"How would I know? You're talking crazy, Chick."

He shoves her aside with the sweep of an arm. Seizes the metal mixing bowl and drives its base through the nearest windowpane, smashing the glass to shards in two blows. Then he pokes his nose out, sniffing like a dog. "Smell it. It's out there. She's out there." He snarls. "If it's the last thing I do, I'm going to find that bitch."

KARALEE, TOO, SMELLS fresh bread on the wind. But she's less certain what it means than Chick seems to be in his delirium.

With slow steps, the three of them leave the kitchen and the Tuberculosis Pavilion, emerging out onto the plaza. The rain has stopped, but fog is rolling in, throwing a wet shroud over everything. They can't see the other buildings, which forces them to feel their way around from memory, Karalee half holding up Estela, whose bad leg drags behind her now as the dead appendage it always threatened to become. She can lift it off the ground only with great effort.

Chick marches ahead, oblivious to their slowness. They stay close to him only because he keeps stopping at short intervals to sniff the air, then readjusts his line of attack to the scent. The fog may be helping in this regard, acting as a magnifier.

Also magnified: the ghostly cries of women and children. All around them, the voices from last night arise, reinvigorated. Their clamor sounds so substantive and so close that Karalee reaches out a few times in an attempt to touch them. But each time, her hand meets nothing but wet air. When Chick pauses longer than usual, she puts the Nikon camera to her eye and peers through the viewfinder. Seeing unmistakable shadows around them shaped like human forms, she snaps a few pictures with the shutter set slow, if only to test whether her eyes are playing tricks.

"What are you doing?" Estela asks.

"Making a visual record."

"Of the fog?"

After fifteen minutes of nearly blind groping, they arrive at an area where the distinct aroma of baking bread smells stronger than ever. "It's here," Chick says, peering through mist at a brick wall just coming into view. "What building is this?"

Karalee shrugs to hide her reluctance. She doesn't see any good resulting from this chase. But Estela spots the base of a smokestack and points. "It's the crematorium."

"That doesn't make any sense," Karalee says, but in a perverse way it makes perfect sense. And it's hard to argue with the intensity of the smell. As they close in on the building, it becomes clear that Estela guessed right.

They work their way closer and enter through a partially open door to the front hall, which leads to an anteroom that gives way to the heart of the building. A faint glow emanates from the doorway, and warmth radiates from that direction. It feels good on Karalee's face.

They sense a presence, but inch forward in defiance of their own trepidation. Karalee, considering Chick's argument, now allows for the possibility that he's right about Mary's identity. But if he is right, what does that mean for the future prospects of George A. Soper's great-granddaughter on this island?

"I wonder whether it's Josh in there," Estela says, barely disguising the desperation in her voice.

"What the hell would Josh be doing baking bread?" Chick snaps.

"What would anyone be doing baking bread in a crematorium?" says Estela.

"If it's the only place with a working oven," Karalee speculates, "it's completely logical."

Her remark goes unanswered. In thirty-six hours, they have become accustomed to bizarre exigencies. Homeless Mary digs in soil where thousands suffered. The Sewer Rats, for their part, press on with their desperate adventure among the empty husk of historical misery that Mary calls home. Such is the nature of abandoned North Brother Island, or so Karalee rationalizes. The island persists in making its demands. What exactly is going on with Estela and Chick, she can't say. They are sick for real—anyone could see that. But they are not poisoned. She knows this because she ate all the same food they did, and she feels fine. Then again, hasn't she always felt fine? When eight of every ten students had chickenpox in her elementary school, she remained unscathed. When the flu tore through her high school, laying half the class on their backs, she didn't miss a beat. When she traveled with her family to Central America and her parents both got food poisoning, she spent a boring day poolside, unaffected, waiting for them to recover. More troubling, now that she thinks about it, she can't recall ever having so much as a sniffle. Well, she's lucky that way. Some people are, right?

Her left ear itches like crazy at the site of the scar. So, there's that—not complete bodily perfection—but then again, this effect was induced by a physical blow, not a bug. She scratches at the scar, feels her nails dig too deep, inflicting mild pain. Forces herself to stop. But it's getting harder. She licks her dirty finger—tastes salt and a pleasant bitterness—and rubs saliva along the scar.

When she refocuses her attention, they are standing in the middle of the main crematorium space, staring through the dim glow at a line of ovens. Karalee expects to see Mary, but she isn't here. She notices something else.

"Listen to that," she says.

As they approached this building, the voices outside grew in volume. Now, within its walls, utter silence prevails. Karalee hears only Estela wheezing in the warm air. They are holding each other, Estela's urgent grip clawing into Karalee's arm. Even Chick has lost his nerve and eased closer to them.

Karalee's joints strain under Estela's tugging, as burdensome as dead weight. Chick's legs are trembling. From fever or fear—she doesn't know.

"What the hell is this? There's fire inside here," he says in the tone of an accusation. He shakes himself free of his friends, walks six steps to the wall, and touches the nearest oven door.

SEVEN RUSTED DOORS hang in a line across the brick crematorium wall like cast-iron sentinels. One door is missing, a pair of sledge tracks disappearing into a dark maw. Another, frozen open, cants off its hinges, clearly nothing burning inside, unless this mysterious fire burns black.

Chick has approached the closed door to the far right. He holds his knuckles against it, and the back of Karalee's tongue turns cottony. But after five long seconds of contact, he shakes his head. Cold. He steps to the next door. Touches it. His shoulders relax. Cold. The third is broken. He skips it. Touches the next. Cold.

Karalee releases a breath. Sensing greater safety, she and Estela ease toward the wall of ovens. Chick touches the fifth door and quickly withdraws his hand. "It's warm," he whispers. Estela has the flesh of a knuckle clamped between her teeth. Karalee squeezes her other hand tight.

Chick grasps the handle to the oven door. Time unfolds with unbearable slowness as he inches the door open, the sledge inside gradually revealing itself. When there are four inches of clearance, he peeks over the top of the door, his face neutral and inscrutable, Estela and Karalee clutching at one another. Then Chick breaks into a wide smile and pulls harder at the door with its attached sledge. As it opens, a gust of heat hits their faces, carrying the strong and distinct aroma of fresh baking bread.

He laughs—half in satisfaction at his rightness, half at the escape from his own fear—and rubs an eye with the knuckle of his forefinger, then runs a hand through his ponytail. In the dim orange light and with the release of tension, he almost looks himself again.

Estela and Karalee step up and peer over the door into the sledge. There's a large and beautiful loaf of bread inside, well tanned, nearly ready, illuminated by a fire they can't directly see. Karalee, her stomach growling, wishes she could take a bite out of it right now. Estela, one hand resting on Karalee's shoulder, giggles so like a little girl that Karalee can see all her worries physically taking flight.

"She's just a cook." Estela sighs. "A good cook. I wish I could bear to eat." She lays a hand across her chest and swallows with a frown.

Chick, too, has already begun to look pale again. He says, "We didn't come for the bread. We came for Mary. Where is she?" He shuffles a step and spins around, but no one has approached them from behind.

It is hot beside the open oven, oppressive to Karalee. She goes to the oven door in order to close it, grips the handle, and shoves. But it doesn't slide as easily as she expected, so she plants her feet, employs her legs, and puts her shoulder into it. After applying great effort, and with the sledge guides shrieking, she finally gets it closed.

The hot air dissipates immediately, and she welcomes relative coolness for the first time since the weather changed yesterday. Leaning against the wall between oven doors, she runs her hands through her hair and takes a deep breath. But as she steps to the side of one oven door, her butt brushes against the next. Surprisingly, she finds that it is also warm to the touch.

She looks to her friends, their attention drifting, illness beginning to have its way with them. *Where is Josh?* she thinks. *Where the hell is Josh?* In school, she learned about an intellectual approach called Occam's razor: no more assumptions should be made than are absolutely necessary. So to assume that Mary is Typhoid Mary and that she had anything to do with Gerard's horrific death and that Josh, now . . . She can't bear the thought. Occam—smart guy. More famous than George A. Soper will ever be. And yet, the tug—the tug on her. It comes from George, as George tugged on her father. *Soper Soap Cleans Cleanest!* What foolishness. Occam can be right or George can be right—not both. Karalee can be right or her father can be right.

Chick has his hands on his hips, jaw set, spinning around and around, as if looking for someone to hit.

"There's nothing in this oven drawer," Karalee says quietly, fingers resting on the handle.

"What?" asks Estela, pale-faced, sheened with sweat. She teeters on her feet.

"There is nothing in this drawer, right? Nothing bad. There was bread in the other, but there's nothing bad in here. Right, Estela, right?"

"I don't know. I have to lie down." Estela collapses onto her butt, crumpling onto the dust-covered floor.

"There's nothing. There will be nothing. There can't be anything." Karalee repeating it like a mantra as she grasps the oven-door handle and gives a firm tug. But the sledge resists—everything so disused and rusty around here.

"The oven is empty. Or more bread baking. That's it: more bread."

The next time, she pulls with all her might, and the door springs free with a screech, nearly knocking her off her feet. Her throat spasms as she recovers her balance and looks down into the sledge.

"More bread baking. More bread. More bread. Oh, God. Oh, God Almighty."

Karalee's stomach somersaults into her suddenly dry throat. She is looking down upon the scorched remains of a young man whose hair has been reduced to cinders and whose broiled lips and nose have peeled back to expose the hard whiteness of a grimacing skull.

She wishes they hadn't come here—to this room, to this island. For the first time ever, she wishes beyond doubt that she were anyone but the great-granddaughter of the man who set these events in motion. Anything but what she knows in her sinking heart. Yet the black-framed eyeglasses melted onto the face on the sledge reveal inescapable truth. And the twitch in her gut confirms for Karalee what her eyes refuse to acknowledge: that the monstrosity she now looks down upon once walked the earth—walked the earth just this morning—as her dear friend Josh.

KARALEE FEELS HER mouth stretched wide open with her vocal cords vibrating, but she doesn't know what, if anything, emerges from the convulsions that run in waves through her chest. Beside her, Chick releases a shuddering groan, and Estela's earsplitting shriek sends tremors into her soft tissue.

Then they are running—across the crematorium, through the anteroom, out the entrance, and into the night, encased in fog. It makes no sense. They are fleeing a corpse. But they run anyway, so shot through with adrenaline that Estela's dead leg has come alive and she moves with the grace and urgency of a sprinter.

Soon they scuffle blind in the fog, bereft of any sense of direction. Everywhere around them, the voices of spirits cackle and chitter and carp and wail—individual plaintiffs who share a common indictment against all the living. They harrow Karalee. Pursue her whether she runs forward or shuffles sideways or hugs herself for protection. They are suffocating. She can't breathe, feels as if they will drown her in their sorrowful clamor. Chick and Estela bat at their own ears, frantic to make the voices go away. They whirl and flail at the thick air to no avail.

Somehow, through the chaos, together the three survivors arrive at the edge of the woods, falling with their backs against the trunk of a large sycamore tree in an attempt to protect their flanks. The shrieking voices persist, human but not human, like the cries of screech owls and hyenas and foxes and—yes—living persons from the *General Slocum*, all melded together, and the anguish on Chick's and Estela's faces is writ so large that Karalee can see it in the dark. It glows with its own horrid energy.

When she turns her attention to herself, she finds that her bottom is wet. She has pissed her pants but doesn't care, vaguely recalls that she's wearing a bathing suit underneath her soiled shorts. They are all three wet and foul-smelling, the mist clinging to them, augmenting the animal musk of their fear.

"We're getting off this island," Chick says through clenched teeth. "We owe it to Josh and Gerard to make our way out of here even if it ki—" He chokes on the end of the phrase, his words expiring but not his body. Not yet.

Nor does he cry, Karalee notices. None of them are crying. They have passed through sorrow and fear to the pure imperative of survival.

Estela says, "Okay. Okay. Okay. Okay." Rallying herself.

"We're safe if we stick together," Chick says. "The bitch only picked them off when they were alone."

Karalee flinches when she hears Chick call Mary that, although she knows it's all horrible. He proved himself right about some things she'd rather not dwell upon just now. And yet she can't bear to denigrate the terrible woman. "If we couldn't escape during the day," she says, "we can't escape now in the dark."

"We wasted all that time fretting over Gerard." Chick balls his hand into a fist and snarls. "We have to give one hundred percent to get out of here."

"Common cause. Sewer Rats," Estela mutters.

"Not thinking straight won't help," Karalee says. "There's nowhere to go tonight. If we swam for it, we'd drown."

"We'll light the whole place up, like Josh wanted to do. Take a match to it."

"No!" Her mind's churning. "Everything's wet right now."

The voices rise around them. Chick grabs his ears and covers them like an overwhelmed child.

Karalee reaches across Estela's chest and takes ahold of his forearm to command his attention. "It's quieter inside. We have to go back to the ward for the night."

"No." He drops his hands and flinches at the cry of a banshee stabbing through the woods. "She'll find us."

"She'll find us out here! No walls to protect us, and she knows the terrain better. Inside, we won't be easily separated. You said yourself she won't harm us if we stick together."

Karalee senses his mind working. He grimaces. "The lab. If there's an antidote—antibiotics or whatever—they could be there."

"Not far from the ward."

"Okay," he concedes. "Which way?"

Karalee is the only one with a full set of wits intact. Even through the thick mist, she thinks she can lead them back. She scratches the scar on her left ear, and the act gives her the sensation of removing rime from a window. She doesn't feel quite herself, but not because of the sickness that ails Chick and Estela. More like a growing sense of purpose that she can't yet identify. But she feels it clarifying.

THE MOON OF last night is a vivid but distant memory. Out in the foggy woods, Karalee has lost all sense of time. They flail in the murkiness for hours—or for minutes that seem like hours—harried without mercy by the spirit voices, urging one another forward when they fall, until a sprawling brick building finally looms into view. The Tuberculosis Pavilion. Has she ever felt so relieved to lay eyes on a pile of clay?

She leads Chick and Estela stumbling and wheezing and dry heaving through the door and across the lobby and up the stairs and down the hall in the direction of the familiar ward. But as they close in on it, Chick hooks her hip and spins her around.

"Not so fast. You promised a look at the lab. We need the cure." He looks at Estela, who, flagging, nods with her eyes rolling back.

"Of course," Karalee says.

It is pitch dark. They no longer have Gerard's lighter or Chick's borrowed candle to light their way, and Karalee's camera flash is long dead. They must feel their way back down the hall and around the bend, opening doors to several empty rooms until they finally rediscover the laboratory.

In the presence of counters and dry sinks and disused Bunsen burners, Chick and Estela rally. They rifle through drawers and cabinets, groping for anything that might suggest a bottle or a package of pills, probing the shapes of their finds with their fingertips, and—if they seem promising— holding them up an inch from their noses for careful study. Just in time, the darkness outside has begun to relent, the moon glowing through low-lying clouds. Little light reaches them, but with their eyes now acclimated to darkness, it is enough to function.

When he's searched every drawer, Chick spreads his gleanings on the counter, sorting through, pushing to the floor that which is useless to him. Eventually, he pauses, holding up to the moonlight a glass sleeve with an old red-and-yellow label. "Holy shit. I found the grail. Against all odds, I have it!"

"What is it?" Karalee asks.

"Prontosil, a sulfur-based drug, the original antibacterial."

"And it's still good?"

He shakes the contents into his palm. "We're going to find out. Let's see. There are a dozen pills here. Four for each of us."

Karalee shakes her head. "You guys take it. I'm not sick."

He shrugs and chokes down half the pills dry, passing the rest to Estela, who accepts them absently and swallows, not taking her eyes off something she found in the cabinet: the old tin specimen box that Gerard originally identified.

"Look," she says. Two of the six test tubes have their seals freshly broken. "Someone's been into them recently, and their contents are mostly gone."

Karalee sidles up next to her. She lifts one of the test tubes to see for herself. Its cork stopper is only half depressed, and a ring of wax has clearly separated from the rim. The glass is fogged or dirty, but she can make out the residue of a liquid that's the color of concentrated tea.

Chick grabs it from her and peers into it. "The very thing. Mary Mallon's disease." He drops the test tube into its slot and pushes away the box in disgust.

Outside, the voices rise in a wailing wave.

Inside, somewhere downstairs, Karalee hears movement.

THERE IS ONLY one place in the pavilion that still represents relative safety and familiarity, and that is the ward where they slept. With Chick and Estela in tow, Karalee races as fast as her unwell friends allow, down the rubble-strewn hallway and through the open doorway.

Inside, they lurch to an abrupt halt, holding one another, standing shoulder to shoulder. Cots and mattresses and pillows lie strewn about as if tossed by a tornado, and those few windowpanes not previously broken hang in shards.

"Well," Chick says, breathing heavily, placing his hands on his hips, and barking out a forced laugh at the absurdity of this safety zone, "no more treats on the pillow."

They gather their strength long enough to push and toss the cots into the doorway, where the items settle into a tangled pile—an improvised fence. Then they grab the mattresses and shove them into the gaps as best they can, using the pillows to block the smaller spaces. As a barricade, it's fools' work—anyone can easily shove a pillow aside—but it serves to cocoon them in the room. Out of sight if not out of the madwoman's mind.

The moment they're done, Chick falls to the floor, his back against their makeshift barrier. At his direction, Estela takes up a similar position against the sealed door across the room, so if someone attempts to pry it open, she'll feel it. Karalee sits against the wall between them, under the line of windows.

She twists and looks over her shoulder into the sky. "It's clearing a little bit. Not so foggy. I can see glimpses of the moon. It's full—or nearly so. Like last night."

"Not clear. Clear. Not clear. Clear." Chick gives an exhausted shrug. "Lotta good that moon did to protect us last night. Maybe the opposite. Maybe without visibility, Gerard doesn't end up at the tower."

"At least we can see three feet in front of us now," Estela says quietly, all the energy drained from her voice. "It did help you find the pills, Chick. Do you think they'll really work?"

"Have faith, Estela. They'll make a dent. We need only twelve more hours of strength. By morning, we'll fetch some matches from the pantry and light this place up. Then the boats will come. They'll rescue us and grab ahold of Mary."

"Like they got her last time?" Karalee asks. "With overwhelming force?"

"Until then, we'll have to be careful," Chick continues, ignoring her. "There's nothing more dangerous than a cornered animal."

Karalee looks down at her feet. They're bare, she notices for the first time. Sliced up and scraped, with black filth mortared into the cuts. She must have run right out of her sneakers hours ago. How strange that she didn't notice. But hysteria drove her then. Now that she's calm, her feet throb and burn. Her neck hurts where her camera strap has been rubbing all day. Her right hip aches where the Nikon kept bouncing against it. She lifts the strap over her head, can't resist snapping a picture of the moon veiled behind clouds. Her roll of film has only two shots left. She lovingly sets the camera down by her feet and looks up, assessing her companions.

Sweet, vibrant Estela is a shell of her former self.

Chick—she is growing to hate. That ponytail . . . the hippie look . . .

his intellectual airs—they're just a disguise to hide his misogyny. In complete exhaustion, she does see this one thing clearly: If he ever attempts to touch her sexually again, she will kick him in the balls.

She has never done violence to anyone, but in a self-defense class she once attended they taught her to go straight for the testicles, to hit a man where he's most vulnerable. She wonders whether Mary Mallon ever attempted to kick George A. Soper in the balls. Certainly, notwithstanding the different moral codes of that era, it seems not at all out of character. Also, she wonders, as her mind drifts, whether any of the few surviving women of the *General Slocum* tried to kick Captain Van Schaick in that most vulnerable spot. Negligent, criminal, despicable Captain Van Schaick. If he didn't have it coming, who did?

A phrase from her college Shakespeare floats up: "murder most foul." Yes. The very proper Knickerbocker Steamship Company murdered those women and children just as very proper society murdered Mary Mallon's hopes, turned her into the walking dead. What difference, really, between her life on North Brother and that of the ghosts?

And Gerard? And Josh? a voice in her head counters. *They weren't Captain Van Schaicks. What did they do to earn what they got?* But as soon as she formulates the question, she sees that they were not without fault from Mary's perspective. They intruded upon her territory, not the other way around. Did they have any right to expect no consequences for their trespass? Do any of those who set foot here?

The voices—the spirit voices. She lets her eyes lose focus, and they recede into background noise, like the chirping of frogs on a pond, only more sinister. They felt deeply threatening during the frantic retreat through darkness and fog, but now they invoke less fear in Karalee. And she is so tired. She struggles to keep her eyes open, looks to her friends, who sit limp and expended. Allows her eyelids to flutter closed, just for a minute.

And she dreams.

Not any dream. *The dream.* The nightmare more vivid than ever.

She is a small child in a diaper sitting on the linoleum kitchen floor. "Stinky diaper," she hears her mother say. The diaper has leaked. Kiki stuck her fingers in it, using the mess to finger-paint on the floor. Brown clouds. Brown flowers. Bad girl. Bad Kiki. Her father looms. When she first catches sight of him, she hears the jingle in her mind. Sitting in the car, the big Buick, they once listened for it on the radio. *Soper Soap Cleans Cleanest!* "Hear the jingle, Kiki? Hear it?" When she giggled, he said, "Oh, you'll be a Soper through and through!"

But her father isn't wearing the smile he had when the jingle came on. Bad Kiki. Dirty girl. He is livid, frowning in disgust. Then she's in his hands, moving through air so quickly that it feels as if her stomach gets left behind. She finds herself roughly set down. Squishy in the stinky diaper. In the dog crate. He slams the door with a clatter. And for good measure, as she cries and reaches her little fingers through the wire of the cage, he picks up the whole thing and gives it a good shake, jostling her. He drops it with a jarring crash, setting the cage wire twanging.

Is this only a dream? It seems so real. She is crying, gasping, suffocating. She must escape it, knows she has to wake herself, but she's as helpless as a toddler in a cage. She tries to scream but can't, the scream buried too low in her viscera. With Chick way across the room in one direction and Estela way across the room in the other, who will shake her awake and rescue her?

A scream comes so loud and strident that it sounds unearthly—like something from the depths of hell. It is not Karalee screaming. All at once, she feels an elbow in her chest—Estela sailing into her and sending the camera flying, sliding into the wall to Chick's right with a crash. Karalee has broken Estela's fall. It hurt them both, but it woke Karalee in time to witness a blur of movement that came through the previously frozen door, to see the now-familiar skirt, the collection of quilted rags surging across the room. Two, three, four steps. The living ghoul's face purple with rage. Carving fork poised in the air. Pure hatred in her mismatched eyes.

Chick stirs and looks up just in time to avoid the worst, starts to push himself up off the floor, off center, off kilter. What he sees—what they all see—is a fork-wielding arm arcing down in his direction, inescapable. Karalee hears the air chuff out of him as the fork buries itself in the left side of his chest.

A MOMENT OF astonishment hangs in the air. Mary stands over Chick, puffing, red-faced. With Estela sprawled on the floor, looking broken, Karalee springs to her feet and runs instinctively to crouch at Chick's side. The fork missed his heart, but blood drips down like running tears from the two holes where the tines penetrated. She bites her lower lip and raises a hand to pull the fork out.

"Don't you touch it!" Mary barks. "Let him die! He deserves to die!"

Behind her, Estela has finally, shakily arisen. She scans the room for a weapon and settles on Karalee's Nikon, lying off to the side. In one quick stooping step, she grabs its strap, spins, and swings the heavy camera at Mary's head, but the larger woman anticipates danger and straightens up. The camera bounces off her back but does not scathe her. She yanks the strap from Estela's hand and dashes the camera against the floor.

"You're evil!" Estela cries. "You killed our friends! You made us sick!"

"I killed no one who did not deserve to be killed. Open your eyes, girl. Them boys and this man invaded my island and shattered my peace. They are the ones need to suffer for a change. And to hell with them!"

"We meant you no harm," Chick says, wincing with each breath. "We didn't even know who you were."

"You do now, mister." She raises a hand to him.

"Help me, Kiki!" he shouts.

But Karalee remains in a crouch. It's Estela, instead, who plants her feet and drives her hip into Mary with all her might, knocking her off her mark. Meanwhile, Karalee, finally attempting to shield Chick from Mary's wrath, has jostled the fork free from his chest. He yelps and gasps, but then wheezes: "I'm all right. I think it hit bone."

Karalee feels tears running down her cheeks. Doubt creeps in, her inner resolve torn by the spasm of violence. There she was, minutes ago, working up to hatred of Chick, and here she is, now, attempting to protect him. She squeezes her temples. Outside, the spirit voices rise with savage force.

"Hear them," Mary says, recognizing Karalee's state. "The women and children. They want justice. Don't they deserve justice?"

Estela, her eyes coming back alive, has seized Mary's fork and brandishes it. "Get back! It's not for you to make justice here!"

"If not here—where? This is where they put me. Think, girl, what they did to me—a poor Irish lass from Cookstown, not so different from yourself. A girl who only wanted to make a living cooking and be left alone. Soper!" She spits on the floor, meets Karalee's gaze. "You understand, don't you? I see it in your face. You're not like that man, your ancestor. You're with me."

"I am not with you!" Karalee screams, as much to convince herself as to persuade Mary. She scratches at the scar on her left ear, which itches like mad.

Mary lifts a bushy eyebrow. She grins, showing her snail-shell teeth.

Karalee averts her eyes, her attention disrupted by the sight of her broken camera on the floor. Its back cover has popped off, exposing the undeveloped film inside. She reaches for it and twists the sprockets, begins pulling the film out. Images are visible on the shiny surface—ghostly images. Women and children being consumed in flame. Anguish on their faces.

Her hand goes to her mouth. "Estela! Chick! We need to get out of here."

"You see them," Mary says, eyes wide. "You will always see them."

"No!" Karalee cries, lip trembling. She slings the camera down.

Chick reaches behind him and grabs the leg of a cot and swings the entire thing forward with preternatural force. It smashes into Mary's side and she goes down like an uprooted tree. He seizes another cot with his last reserves of strength and throws it on top of the fallen woman.

"Run!" Estela screams. "Run!"

The ghost voices scream, too. They are in the pavilion, all around them, grinding like a record played backwards. Karalee doesn't understand a word they say, but she feels their anguish to the depth of her soul.

And then, following her friends, she runs.

Mary

HUMILIATED AND LOCKED away, Mary has been. But in all her many years of torment, no one ever raised a hand to strike her. Not her brothers, who all feared her and left her to her own devices. Not Briehof, who would sooner kick the toothy dog than challenge her. Not the police, who overwhelmed her with force during her apprehension but kept their billy clubs by their sides—the only physical harm being the pounding of Dr. Baker's bony ass on her ribs whenever the paddy wagon hit a pothole on the way to the hospital. Not even the brutes who strapped her to a chair and drew her blood.

And of course not Soper, coward of cowards.

She laughs bitterly as she rises, working her arm, nothing broken.

The voices are loud tonight—loud as they have ever been. One stands out. It screeches to life in her presence. The singed hair. The boiled skin. It cradles the blackened boy, Adolf, and drags the skinny limp girl, Friede, behind itself by one arm like a rag doll extracted from a moldering grave and passed through a smoky fire.

"Your bread is burning," Mathilde says.

"No one is hungry anymore."

"There are many things to be hungry for besides bread."

Mary picks up her carving fork, dropped by the Soper girl's friend.

She wipes the tines clean on her shirt, leaving two stripes of blood. "He has an infection. They all have the disease now."

"Not all of them."

"There's a wild card in every deck. With your help, I will finish the game."

"Oh, you're eager for my help now, are you?"

"I'm a loner by nature, Mathilde. But nothing wrong with taking a partner now and then. Where are they?"

"*Verloren.* Lost. Lost on North Brother. The fog thickens at the most inconvenient times, doesn't it? As it did for Dolores. But since when does anything go as planned around here?" Mathilde cackles. "God laughs so hard, his sides are splitting."

She lets go Adolf, who falls to the floor with a thud.

The sound, like a watermelon struck by a mallet, startles Mary and shakes the ground beneath her.

"You didn't know I had that trick," Mathilde says with satisfaction.

The boy doesn't move. "You'd think he'd cry out," says Mary.

"Why would he cry out?" Mathilde snarls. "The boy's long dead."

Karalee

As THEY CROSS the remains of the plaza, Chick grunts with each step and Estela wheezes incessantly. Karalee's heart pounds in her chest and sweat courses down her temples. They feel eyes upon them, but the reconstituted fog stymies all efforts to break free. And Mary is no quitter. She pursues them and will pursue them till the end. Karalee knows this as deeply as she knows anything.

"Hurry!" she shouts over unrelenting ghost voices.

Chick stumbles along, his swagger gone, holding a bloodied hand over his open wound. Estela drags half her body like a heavy sack. When Karalee looks at her full-on, she sees an angry rash blossoming across her chest.

Just yesterday, Karalee had an aversion to dirt. Now she feels the grime on her own soiled clothing and almost relishes it. On a lighter occasion, she thinks, they might joke about how pathetic they all look. But appearance means nothing now. The next hour—if not sooner, she fears—will decide their fate.

A heavy horn sounds over the river. The fog has doubled down, the moon a shy gray orb wrapped in gauze. They are in the vicinity of the greenhouse when they hear a rustling movement through leaves at the edge of the woods.

No rat or rabbit. No small animal. A more substantial presence.

Karalee pushes Chick through the nearest doorway and pulls Estela in after her. Just in time. Something heavy crashes through the fog. Right behind them ring the sounds of metal striking metal and glass breaking. They duck around the next corner and the next, half blind, tripping over clay pots. The greenhouse, shrouded in fog, lit only by the corona of a pale moon, has transformed itself into a hall of mirrors. They pause in one room to catch their breaths and to orient themselves. A shadow looms on the glass behind Chick. At first, Karalee thinks it's one of their own distorted reflections. Then it appears as a ghostly shade, like what she saw through her camera, but now coming into plain view. "You will always see them," Mary said. Karalee discerns a silhouette of the great big carving fork and the shape of a large skillet in the shadow's hand. It is the skillet that comes crashing down, shattering the glass.

Mary hulks through the passageway she just made. Chick flips a pebble-covered table into her path, cutting her off at the knees. And they run again, out the back of the greenhouse, out into the thick night. Out into the woods.

It was hard enough to wend their way through these woods in daylight or during a moonlit night. In the fog, it feels like a futile task, and they struggle to make headway through fallen branches and hanging vines and protruding roots. Karalee, barefoot, feels every twig. Voices call at them from all sides in German and broken English.

"Mommy, where are you!"

"Ich brenne!"

"I can't see!"

"The smoke! The smoke!"

"Kommt hier entlang!"

"To the ladders! This way!"

It is tempting to pick one voice and track it, if only to establish a consistent direction, but Karalee suspects they wish her to follow that impulse. They intend to lead her astray.

Out of sight—behind them or in front of them or beside them, who could tell?—those few left of the Sewer Rats hear Mary in pursuit but can't see her through the fog. She could be a hundred feet away or only two dozen. She might close in at any moment or run them into hiding and besiege them.

It is impossible both to keep quiet and to keep moving at the same time. So they choose speed over quiet, crashing along. In time, they stumble into the clearing with the chopping block. The ax is still embedded there. Chick lays his hands on the handle, but he no longer has the strength to pull it out. He tugs and he tugs, grabbing at the wound in his chest between efforts. Karalee goes over to help. Estela stands lookout, squinting helplessly into the gloom.

Just as they free the ax, Mary emerges from the fog, carving fork in hand, rushing at them with a rustle of fabric. Chick has a weak grip on the ax handle. He goes to raise his weapon but drops it to the ground with a cry of pain. A scream of exertion comes from behind, and Estela cracks Mary square across the back of her head with a tree limb. She falls face forward onto the bare ground, the ax trapped under her, half of its handle protruding.

"Let's go!" Chick says, but Karalee has her eye on the ax. She points. "We could use that."

"I'm not rolling her over to get it," Chick says, stepping back. "She might wake up. She's stronger than all of us put together."

"No, she isn't. Not stronger than me. And no more healthy." Karalee falls to a knee. She takes hold of the ax and slides it free in two pulls, Mary's body twitching with each tug, but not rousing. Now Karalee has the ax handle across her shoulder.

"Kill her!" Chick urges. "Smash her brains in!"

Karalee feels her power ascendant, and she won't be bossed by Chick. She stands trancelike, staring down at the pathetic Mary. Is that all it would take? A blow to the head to save everyone? The ghost voices have fallen silent. The ax handle rests lightly on her shoulder. She is the ancient Minoan goddess, wielding her labrys. She is Lizzie Borden in Fall River, Massachusetts. Karalee lifts the ax over her head and arches her back, but suddenly feels two pinpricks behind her. Jabs from the barbecue fork, still tucked into the band of her shorts. The sensation startles her. She lowers the weapon.

"What are you doing!" Estela says. "She killed Josh! She killed Gerard! Kill her!"

"She's a hundred and thirteen years old," Karalee says. "And she never had a moment of peace in her whole life."

"I'll do it if you won't," Estela says. But she's bluffing. They both know the tree limb tested the limit of her one good arm, and the ax is much heavier.

"We'll use it on the boathouse," Karalee says, breathing deeply, calmly. "We'll get there ahead of her. It's this way."

Suddenly, she knows just where she's going. Ax restored to her shoulder, she turns and walks forward without waiting. Let the weaklings follow at their own pace.

BEHIND HER, KARALEE hears their footsteps but does not turn around. She hears her friends pausing to cough and retch, but she doesn't break stride.

She arrives at the open boathouse door and walks through, peering into the murk. Chick comes up behind her, holding his chest. Estela drags herself to the threshold.

"Close the door," Karalee says.

She and Chick enter while Estela clears debris from the doorway. Estela is bent over, getting the last few branches, when in one vicious motion, a skillet whizzes through the air and smashes into her head, cracking her skull with a sickening snap. The skillet rises again and crashes down once more, exploding Estela's head like a gore-filled melon.

Karalee flinches at Estela's sudden demise, but it prods her into unthinking action, sends her racing back to the door with Chick. They push it closed with all their might, driving Mary back out, screaming ferociously. But the lock is long gone. With Mary pounding away, Karalee has no choice but to stand with one foot on Estela's unmoving body, her heel feeling Estela's ribs as she presses her shoulder against the warped wooden door, jostled by each blow.

"Hold her!" Chick looks around and finds a piece of wood to brace the door closed, wedging one end against the door and the other in a gap of the dock.

With the brace providing more solid resistance, the pounding stops for a moment, Mary reassessing her plan of attack.

Karalee takes the opportunity to hand Chick her ax. "The garage door," she says.

"I can't lift it above my head. That bitch—"

"Man up, Chick. Swing sidearm if you have to. Just go!"

Without further protest, he runs and mounts the bow of the Slick-Craft and directs the ax in a low arc at the garage door. With the first blow, he takes its measure. With the second, he breaches one of the panels, catching the axhead, struggling to tug it free while the boat rocks below him in splashing water.

The door begins vibrating again under Mary's onslaught, and Karalee presses her shoulder against it, her bones rattling, blows from Mary's skillet shaking the boathouse to its foundation and beginning to yield cracks in the wood panels, through which she probes now and then with her sharp fork, just missing Karalee's arm and midsection on several occasions.

Estela is dead—has to be with her brains spilling out—but she is still warm under Karalee's feet. When the pounding pauses again, Karalee quickly stoops and pulls the body aside in order to mount a better defense. With the board holding, she finds a piece of split wood and wedges it under the kickplate, pounding it into place with the sore heel of her right foot.

"Chop faster," she tells Chick over her shoulder.

He is making nice progress now with the garage door. Having broken the integrity of the crosspieces, he manages to get several horizontal slats to fall away under the force of gravity. Invigorated by his success, he gains strength, now able to lift the ax higher, although he still cries out in pain with each blow. Seeing that the aluminum tracks are holding in place what's left, Chick turns the axhead around and takes a mighty swing to knock the door loose.

At that moment, Karalee thinks she hears the blow and its metallic echo at the same time. But the second sound turns out to be Mary's cast-iron skillet, hitting against the outside hinges. *Ping! Ping!* All sounds synchronizing. Karalee had an idea of what to do, but now it's gone out of her head, the metallic vibration bringing her up short. It rings at a frequency that at once feels familiar and terrifying. The voices join it in concentrated wailing, rising to a resounding buzz, and that merges with her memory of the sound of the green bottle flies and the sound from her nightmares—the sound that the dog cage makes after her father gives it a shake and a drop. Vibrating—it won't stop vibrating. *Dirty girl.*

Chick is smashing at the aluminum guide, now loose—*ping! ping! ping!*—the boat rocking beneath him, the water plashing. As if she senses his progress, Mary redoubles her efforts, batting at the door with increasing violence, cracks forming, plunging her carving fork through those cracks, just missing Karalee, who feels frozen in place, lost.

In a minute, Chick will have the garage door down. Karalee will have to find her way across the dock and into the boat. Still holding the shaking door, she's glancing over her shoulder to assess the boat when a burned and rotting woman rises up from the water, fixating Karalee's attention. She wears a soot-stained and tattered woolen dress, pleated at the waist. A blackened ceramic silhouette pendant hangs around her neck by a melted gold chain. On one side of her head, the dark hair is burned off, exposing bloody and blistered skin from the side of her skull to the drooping left corner of her mouth. She has no eyelashes and only one eyelid, and the whites of her eyes are rheumy and bloodshot. Karalee should not be able to see this level of detail in the poor light, but she does see it. In a heavy German accent, the woman says, "Listen, girl. Not all nightmares are dreams."

She smiles cruelly, and Karalee shudders, thinking of Estela lying there dead, noting the smell of electricity in the air, as right before a lightning storm, and the taste of copper at the edges of her tongue. She forces her attention back to the disintegrating door.

"Almost there, Kiki." Chick huffs, swinging frantically but with great purpose. With three more grunting swings, the remains of the garage door collapse into the water in a sinking heap. Chick swings low once more, and the ax goes flying from his hands into the fog that now rolls along the water and invades the boathouse. He jumps into the boat and attempts to start the motor, but it won't even click, battery long dead.

The door Karalee still holds closed against Mary is almost in splinters now, skillet and fork easily passing through gaping holes, Karalee dekeing and ducking, her hands shifting from one door stile and rail to another. Through the cracks, she can see Mary's mouth foaming spittle, her face deep purple with a lifetime of fury.

Chick jumps to the dock, runs down the ramp, splashes through the water, seizes the canoe paddle from the wall, and returns to the boat, using the paddle to clear the last of the obstruction. Then he jumps aboard, leans out, and frantically unties the ropes. Rotted, they come free easily, and the SlickCraft begins to drift forward.

"Kiki! Hurry! She's free!"

Karalee looks over her shoulder in desperation. With the door giving way, she doesn't know what to do.

Chick leaves the drifting boat and runs to her side. He tugs her arm, but when she shakes him off, he turns to batting against Mary's skillet and fork with his oar, slowing the onslaught.

The taste of copper is strong. Karalee feels the ghost voices as a vibration shaking every sinew of her body. In a single motion, she lets go of the door and Chick steps up and puts his hands flat against what's left of it, arms extended. She snatches the paddle from him, jogs past him, and jumps into the drifting boat. Immediately, she uses the paddle to push off harder, the boat now approaching the open garage door. Chick, seeing her progress, leaves the side door and takes a running dive into the boat as Mary bursts into the boathouse, her face wild, her mouth gritted with revenge.

But they are free. They are only a few feet from free.

Then the boat lurches, Karalee feeling sudden resistance against her paddle. She dunks it over the bow, feeling for the problem, but they're obstructed from behind. Chick, in his haste, missed one of the lines. Although mostly rotted, it has managed to snag them.

Right about the spot where Karalee saw the German woman rise from the water.

"Not all nightmares are dreams."

Soper Soap Cleans Cleanest!

Dirty girl. Dirty girl in the dog cage. Her father hitting her mother in the kitchen. Not a dream. None of it a dream. It all happened for real. The ghosts all around them now, emerging out of the rolling fog—they're real, too.

Chick reaches out across the gunwale to untie the last rope from its cleat. In seconds he has it loose, but as he withdraws, a large fork whips down, impaling his hand to the dock. He cries out and twists around to look at her. "Kiki?"

"Don't call me that. Only my father calls me that."

She loosens her grip on the barbecue fork handle as Mary descends upon Chick, striking with great violence at his head and shoulders with her cast-iron skillet, stabbing him in the neck with her carving fork. Karalee feels a jolt of electricity run through her, spasm along the paths of her nerves. She has a tight grip on the paddle, her arms moving of their own volition as she brings it down upon Chick's head. She wants to resist this impulse, but it feels so good. Better than good. It comes not just from the ghosts or from this sudden, unaccountable impulse to protect Mary once and for all. It comes from deep within her. It is one anger, rising up. Hers and Mary's. Embracing the feeling, she swings the paddle with increasing determination, raising it high and bringing it down upon Chick with ruthless ferocity.

Even once Chick lies unmoving, Karalee continues to batter at him, losing herself to the purity of her own fury until Mary rests a hand on her shoulder, and Karalee comes back to herself. She looks up, and the ghost woman floats over the boardwalk, staring at her, looking gratified. She has two children at her side and gathers them to her.

When all three disappear into the fog that now fills the boathouse, Karalee must appear lost, for Mary begins to speak.

"You and me—we were just going," she says. "You want to go, yes, girl?"

"More than ever."

Karalee lifts Chick's legs and swings him off the boat as Mary Mallon steps aboard. Behind her hip, tied to her waist, Mary carries the tin box filled with her disease. She sets it down on the bench in the back of the boat.

Karalee, using the paddle, pushes off this time without obstructions and steers the SlickCraft into the fog, relishing the sound of moving water that accompanies their progress. In a few moments, they are out in the midst of the river, and she feels a shift as the current wrests them into its womb, the force of Hell Gate grabbing hold of their boat, carrying it forward with more strength than it ever lent the *Flagellum* or—for that matter—the *General Slocum*. The boat doesn't need Karalee's help anymore. She lifts her oar out of the water and rides with the current, wind moving through her hair.

Behind them, North Brother Island glows with burning spirits, forming fiery rings in the mist that cast light on the boathouse and on the gables of the Victorian buildings—on the smokestacks and the unearthly central atrium cresting the tree line by the Tuberculosis Pavilion. Then, all at once, everything on the island recedes into the fog.

On their little boat, the women speak not a word. All about them, the lights from Manhattan and other islands and the mainland refract in the mist. It might make for a nice photograph, if Karalee still had her camera, but she won't allow herself to miss it. The scar on her left ear no longer itches. Her shoulders droop in relaxation, and cheer fills her heart at the prospect of leaving North Brother to its rotten history. At leaving behind Chick and Josh and Gerard and even Estela, too, poor Estela.

Beside her, she discerns Mary's proud profile and thinks of that picture taken in the ward generations ago, how it called to a young woman from the depths of history.

The fog hangs even thicker now, visibility near zero over their bow, but she finds it hard to worry about that. They are floating free, the current their only guide. Away. Away.

Mary wears a placid look on her face for a long minute. Then her mismatched eyes open wide, and Karalee whips her head around to see what she's seeing. Only then does the deafening charge of the tugboat horn explode upon them, its deep vibrations shaking the chambers of their hearts.

Panicked, Karalee reaches for the oar and fumbles with it in the dark. But by the time she gets ahold of it, she can feel their boat tipping over, a wake swamping them.

At once, the snub-nosed bow of the tugboat crests their gunwales like a tower rising from nothingness.

Black is the last thing Karalee sets eyes upon. Blackness out of the blackness.